I0829020

Originally published as Weathering in the Fragile Beings collection.

Weathering

New Protectorate Stories: Volume One: Book Three

Abigail Kelly

Author's note

Weathering is a standalone novella within the wider *New Protectorate Series* and can be read as such. A full reading list and character directory can be found at abigailkkelly.com. Content warnings can also be found there, as well as in backmatter of this book, alongside a glossary.

~Abigail

Full Series List

Glow - novella
Astray - novella
Weathering - novella
Consort's Glory - novel
Empire - novella
Courtship's Conquest - novel
Strike - novella
Vital - novella
Burden's Bonds - novel
Kohl - holiday novella
Faraway - novella
Sanguine - novella
Devotion's Covenant - novel
Valor's Flight - novel

The United Territories and Allies

ESTABLISHED 1917

The United Territories and Allies
Current borders (2044) established
in the 1917 Peace Charter.

Member territories share a common currency and many laws, but maintain individual sovereignty. Each territory holds representation in the UTA Congress and Court, found in the United Neutral Zone.

For those unafraid to seek out the lonely

Chapter One

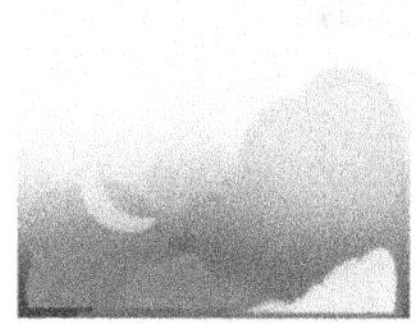

February 2045 - San Francisco, The Elvish Protectorate

FROM THE DESK OF ELISE SASINI, FREELANCE JOURNALIST FOR *THE SAN FRANCISCO LIGHT* & INTERNATIONAL BESTSELLING AUTHOR OF *A GOLDEN LAND: THE UNVARNISHED HISTORY OF SAN FRANCISCO'S ELVISH TAKEOVER*:

Dear Ms. Sasini,

We are so excited about your proposal! You're right — it is well past time someone tracked down the story behind all those social feed pics and urban legends. I can't wait to see what you do with the story! If you need any resources from our research team, let me know. Good luck!

Best wishes,

Dorothy Fan

Non-Fiction Editor at West & Cape Publishing

Penguin Random House LLC

P.S. Say hi to your dad for me! He owes me a damn manuscript!!

~

Elise was an extremely lucky woman.

Only incredible good fortune could explain how she'd managed to secure the best view of San Francisco for nothing more than a signed copy of her father's latest book and a tiny bump in her rent.

Normally, an apartment with a view like hers would be snatched up before she could slide her application into the building manager's inbox, but through a series of unremarkable miracles, she'd learned that the previous tenant was moving out and that the landlord happened to be a huge fan of her father's work.

Elise didn't feel a lick of guilt over bribing her new landlord, either. In San Francisco, you did what you had to do to get a good apartment. She'd lived in the city her entire life, just as her father, Bob Sasini, had. She knew when to move and when to grease the wheels a little to get what she wanted.

Tucking her legs underneath her, Elise sighed with unrestrained pleasure at the sight of the glittering mass of urban life sprawled far below her. The bedroom window she gazed out of overlooked the entirety of downtown San Francisco and beyond, to the black stretch of dangerous water of the Bay and the glowing beacon of Solbourne Tower perched on Treasure Island.

There were only a handful of small apartment buildings scattered this high on the hills, so the streets below her were quiet and lined with scrubby greenery — the only kind that could survive the skin-stripping wind that raked through the area on a regular basis.

But the thing she loved most was the fog.

Sitting on the padded window seat by her bed, Elise held her breath as she watched a curtain of pillowy mist creep in from the Bay. Tonight, it held the shape of downy waves.

San Francisco was famous for its fog, but only locals understood that it was not just a veil of mist that blew in from the sea at a moment's notice. It had wildly different shapes and moved unpredictably.

One day, it might roar in from the water in a single mass, a wall of wet white so thick you couldn't see your hand in front of your face. The next day, it could sweep in gently, unspooling around buildings and through streets like tendrils of smoke from a cold fire. It bounced in like a giant's handful of cotton balls, carelessly tossed, or appeared as a wraith in the time between footsteps.

It was part of the spirit of San Francisco — changing constantly, never settling into dull routine. It was beautiful.

It was *alive.*

Elise's pulse quickened. Everyone knew that the fog had a mind of its own, but no one had been able to catch more than a glimpse of the mysterious, ethereal being who lived in the heart of it.

Even her father couldn't tell her what he looked like or what his name was. The elemental was as hard to catch and mercurial as the fog he was born in.

But Elise wasn't a woman to back down from a challenge.

Born to one of the most legendary crime reporters in the UTA and a weather witch mother, she didn't let her curiosity lie flat and lifeless. She followed the threads of her interests until there was nothing and no one left to question.

The fog had been her longest running obsession. Always simmering in the back of her mind, her fascination with the elemental who guarded the city looked for any excuse, any chance to find a foothold in her life.

Now, at long last, she had a reason to follow the fog.

Chapter Two

The ferry responsible for getting Elise to Alcatraz was, to put it mildly, *fucking ancient.*

She clutched the metal railing of the deck as the ferry rocked over another set of white-crested waves. She'd only done the trip once before, but it looked like even twenty years didn't fix her motion sickness.

Elise focused on the gleaming white walls of the Alcatraz Aerie in the distance, hoping it would help her equilibrium. Waves lashed at the jagged rock of the island. Hardy coastal plants and low-lying shrubs clung to the earth around the Aerie, holding on with determined roots to thin soil and brittle stone.

Salty spray coated Elise's cheeks as she stared up at the island and its only structure. White walls and tall towers pockmarked with narrow doors and rickety stairways stretched up from the craggy surface. It was the only place of worship Loft's acolytes claimed in the Bay Area, and it was beautiful in the brutal, unadorned way the god's worshippers were famous for.

The last time she'd been there, a pilgrim had been found dead in the boat house. Her father was sent by *The San Francisco Light* to write about what quickly turned into a snarled case full of jurisdictional squabbling and she'd begged to come along.

She wasn't sure if she felt pride or queasiness when she stepped off of the ferry and onto the dock. Was it a mark of coming full circle, of stepping out of her father's shadow, to chase her own story across the water?

Maybe, but Elise wasn't the overly sentimental type. It was hard to be when you spent your life in the passenger's seat of a crime reporter's car or getting eviscerated by your editor every time you pushed so much as a sticky note past him.

She was a dogged sort of witch with a goal. Seasickness certainly wouldn't deter her from getting what she was after.

Hitching her overnight bag over her shoulder, Elise adjusted the old, faded baseball cap over her eyes to block out some of the glare bouncing off of the water. She and her handful of fellow passengers, mostly gaunt-faced pilgrims, hurried off of the dock and onto the wide concrete platform below the haunting structure of the Aerie. A dizzying set of stairs linked the platform with the structure, but she knew many of the pilgrims didn't bother with them.

Most who sought succor in the cold arms of Loft were those people who lived and died in their domain — the sky. Harpies, winged shifters, even the rare dragon or two came as pilgrims to the Aerie. They didn't need the stairs, nor the ferry, for that matter.

She tried not to feel too bitter about that as she began the slow trek up the old, weathered stairs. Her fellow wingless travelers were a quiet bunch behind her. Only the sound of the waves and the whistling breeze of a clear San Francisco day joined the steady beat of their footsteps on the creaky wood.

Salt was heavy in the air. Elise took in deep breaths and savored the scent. Living in the city, it was easy to forget that she spent her whole life no more than a few miles from the cold, hungry ocean. The smell of salt and water didn't travel far beyond the immediate shore, and unless you were in a high rise or at the top of a steep hill, you lost sight of the water almost as soon as you stepped off of the beach.

It was impossible to forget on Alcatraz, though.

The sea sprawled around the rocky island, full of sharks and rip currents and schools of sharp-toothed mermaids. Even when she had her back to the waves, Elise felt the lash of them against the sheer rock and felt the salt on her skin, smelled it in her nose.

It was heady and terrifying, just as Loft and their twin brother, Tempest, was.

Elise wasn't particularly religious, but she wasn't immune to the shiver of awe that ran through her as she stepped under the white washed archway of the Alcatraz Aerie. A single compound, it housed devoted acolytes and pilgrims alike. The feeling of so many souls worshipping in one starkly beautiful, isolated place gave the air a heaviness that settled deep into her marrow.

She wasn't there to worship a capricious god, though.

Following the plain, no-nonsense signs, Elise and her fellow sweaty pilgrims made their way across the courtyard in the center of the compound to the visitor's office.

Inside, the decor was just as stark as the outside. A simple wooden desk sat in the middle of the room. Behind it, a harpy dressed in simple off-white robes sat typing on a projected keyboard, her claws clacking against the unpolished surface of the desk.

Her wings were mottled gray flecked with black, matching the hair she kept in a tight bun at the nape of her neck. When the last of the pilgrims piled in, her black claws stilled just long enough for her to flick gold eyes in their direction.

"Welcome, pilgrims," she trilled. Her tone was dry and professional, but even so, it rang with the beautiful notes of a full-blooded harpy. Scanning the clear, razor-thin screen in front of her, she explained, "The ten AM arrivals have been assigned nests twelve through sixteen of the eastern tower. They are all the same, so do not disrespect this sacred place by squabbling over who gets what."

The harpy reached for something behind her desk before she placed four pamphlets down. "Those are maps. Take them or don't. Meals are at eight, noon, and six. Eat them or don't. Communal showers are available in all towers. Water is strictly regulated on the Aerie, so you will get exactly four minutes of showering time. Use it wisely."

Elise swiped one of the pamphlets off the desk and, giving the harpy a nod, moved behind the small group to head towards the door. Someone piped up to ask about what happened if they were to miss a meal, but she didn't need to stay to hear the rest of the harpy's lecture.

She wasn't staying for days of mediation or religious contemplation in the high rookeries, nor terse discussion with the acolytes.

Elise was there to catch a glimpse of a rumored visitor.

Following her map, which was printed on cheap recycled paper in black and white — the acolytes of Loft were a *no frills* bunch even when it came to paper — she found the nests assigned to her group. They were little more than featureless alcoves built into the sides of the spiraling towers connected by staircases and landings that jutted out from the building.

Each level had its own bathroom, but that was the extent of the amenities. The walkways and stairs were exposed to the elements. Only a thin metal railing separated pilgrims from an ugly fall onto the rocks and waves below. The nests themselves were only slightly better off, as they had narrow wooden doors to keep the elements at bay.

Choosing the nest farthest away from the bathroom so she wouldn't hear people coming and going at all hours, Elise ignored her protesting leg muscles and stepped inside.

They really take the "no luxury, only contemplation" bit seriously, she thought, examining the cot on the far side of the room and the bare plaster walls. A single light fixture built into the far wall above the cot illuminated the tiny, windowless space. The sound of gulls calling filtered through the thin wooden door behind her.

Seeing as there was no other choice, Elise shrugged off her bag and took a seat on the cot. She used her forefinger to flick off her baseball cap and stretched out her aching legs.

As someone who spent her entire life wearing down the soles of her shoes on the San Francisco hills, she counted herself as pretty fit. But the stairs of the Aerie were built by people who didn't care about comfort or ease of use. If anything, they went out of their way to do the exact opposite of those things.

Running the fingers of one hand over the bumps of her hasty braid, Elise slid her tablet out of her bag and pulled up her notes. Her stomach felt light, full of fluttering wings. The thrill of the hunt combined with all the exertion made her heart race.

Finally, she could begin.

Chapter Three

As far as Elise could uncover, no one knew the fog's name. Everyone knew his birthday, though.

April sixteenth, 1906. Five o'clock in the morning.

It was the deadliest m-event in the twentieth century, and coming at the tail-end of the Great War, it nearly shattered the very heart of the Elvish Protectorate. There was speculation that all the magic use during combat helped make the m-event, but there was only circumstantial evidence to support the claim.

What they did know for certain was that eyewitnesses claimed the elemental appeared in the rubble of the original Aerie approximately ten minutes after the event. As buildings crumbled from the force of the magical wave and fires raged through San Francisco, he was said to have climbed out of the frigid water and onto the rocks of Alcatraz's bony shore.

After that, information was spotty. Some people claimed they saw him wreaking havoc along the Embarcadero as people scrambled to put out fires and save lives. Some people reported to have seen multiple beings form in the storm of energy that was an m-event. More claimed the whole thing was a new, chaotic weapon developed and deployed by the Iron Chain in a last ditch effort to wipe out the capital of the EVP.

In all Elise's considerable research, she never found a single piece of evidence to corroborate those claims. Going by what they knew today about spontaneous sapient events, the 1906 disaster was just that — a *natural* disaster. Perhaps the war contributed to its severity, but it was almost certainly not something developed or seeded by another territory. It just was.

The only rumors she could even partially substantiate were the ones that claimed Patrol took custody of the elemental for a time, but there was no way to check whether it was true or not. When it came to EVP security, Patrol was under no obligation to disclose its records to the public — particularly during the long, terrible years of the war.

Whatever the case, she knew he began appearing again two years after the disaster. Photographs were rare and almost impossible to authenticate, but Elise had them all, as well as every eyewitness account of a man bleeding out of the fog to rescue a drowning child or to put out a fire or to stop a murder. Once a bad omen, a sighting of the elemental had come to mean safety, *help.*

Part vigilante, part cryptid, all mystery.

One hundred and thirty-nine years, and still, no one knows his name. If the mystery wasn't so very, very tantalizing, Elise would have found it heartbreaking.

No one knew *anything* about the elemental — or, perhaps more likely, those who knew him simply kept his secrets close.

But why?

She contemplated the question all throughout the day as she wandered the Aerie, peeking into meditation rooms and avoiding eye contact with any acolytes that looked a tiny bit too enthusiastic. She was biding her time until nightfall, when the fog typically rolled in off the water. There was the slimmest possible chance she would see the elemental, but being on the island where he was born and rumored to haunt, Elise had far better odds than in the city proper.

Keeping her head down throughout the simple dinner of

barley and mushroom soup and a single fluffy bread roll, she tried to keep her expression properly solemn around her fellow diners in the long, drafty hall.

It wasn't easy, considering she wanted to do nothing more than pace the length of the island until sundown. Elise didn't fear getting in trouble, exactly, but she also didn't care to broadcast her reasons for her own special pilgrimage to the people around her. She suspected they might disapprove of her motives, considering just how little they had to do with their boundless god.

So she waited, and she made polite discussion when absolutely necessary, and she watched the clear February sky bleed into vivid streaks of tangerine and maroon and electric yellow.

As pilgrims and acolytes swooped from perch to perch, heading in for an evening of what Elise could only assume was quiet contemplation of the vastness of Loft's gaze, she sat on a crumbling bit of stonework behind the shrine and watched the fog roll in.

Was he religious? Was that why he was rumored to return to the Aerie?

Elise held her breath as she tracked the creeping mist, her eyes tracing the familiar contours of something always changing, never quite the same as the last time she saw it, but as familiar to her as the lines on her palms. The hunger to know what lay within that beguiling force of nature was a hot, constant burn in her gut.

Maybe it was the weather witch in her that keened for the wildness of discovery, or perhaps it was a lifetime of conditioning from her father to chase down anything and everything that caught her interest. Elise didn't know. At any rate, she wasn't inclined toward introspection.

As soon as the fog reached the farthest edge of the island, Elise hopped off her crumbling seat and made her way back through the archway and down the steps. The light was fading fast and there were no safety lights fixed to a railing — which also didn't exist — to help guide her way down the steep slope, but she didn't think to worry. Her eyes were locked on the jutting dock below, naked without a single boat or the bloated ferry moored to its sides, and where she needed to be when the fog swept in.

Gulls called, and she could hear the sounds of distant horns blaring over the water. Cold wind, so much sharper with its accompanying sting of salt, snapped up to lash her cheeks and the exposed skin of her throat as she half-ran, half-climbed down the steps. She felt no fear as she skidded and nearly stumbled over onto the concrete platform far below her.

The odds that she would encounter the elemental tonight were vanishingly slim, but they carried away all her worries, her mortal fears, and even her common sense with the efficiency of the riptides that coiled like hidden snakes in the water. Her nails were crusted with dirt from gripping the sheer face of the cliff for balance and her breath wheezed in and out of her lungs with the hard scrape of cold air, but Elise didn't notice either discomfort.

The soles of her boots barely made contact with the concrete of the platform before she was launching herself toward the dock. The boathouse was still and dark. Only a single safety light mounted on the lip of its pitiful little awning illuminated the lonely stretch of the dock as darkness dropped like a velvet curtain over the sky.

That happened in San Francisco sometimes: a gorgeous sunset followed by a swift, shockingly dark night. No fuzzy fade, no lavender blush melting into deepest blue. One moment it was all vivid color, and in the next, Darkness had her hands over your eyes.

Elise hadn't spent a whole lot of time outside of the city, so she wondered if it was another peculiarity of her hometown or something that happened everywhere. Not that the darkness scared her. It meant about as much to her as the memory of the murder in the boathouse she jogged by without a glance. It was all just context — set dressing for the stage of her endless curiosity.

The world seemed to quiet as the fog closed in. It muffled the sound of the small, choppy waves and the distant bellowing of horns on massive container ships. Even with all their advanced m-tech, a ship never outgrew its need for horn.

Stopping at the edge of the dock, where old rope coiled around soggy pillars and the smell of brine and oceanic decay clung onto the wet air, Elise unzipped her windbreaker and shrugged it off. She tied it around her waist with a quick knot. Her exertion made her sweat, and that thin sheen of moisture immediately cooled to an uncomfortable layer of tacky coldness on her limbs and throat.

She was dressed unseasonably in an athletic tank top and form fitting black pants, but the cold didn't bother her. She was, after all, a weather witch.

As far as she knew, no one who had ever publicly attempted contact with the elemental had her set of skills. With no other way of tracking him down besides being everywhere in the city at once, Elise planned to try something enormously, deeply stupid.

I'm just going to keep hoping this won't offend him or end up with me smeared on the dock and left for the seagulls, she thought, shaking out her arms and legs with a quick little jiggle.

Truly, what harm could it do? Her chances that he was actually close enough to notice her minor meddling were greater on Alcatraz, but not exactly *stellar.* In all likelihood, she would do little more than waste her evening in the cold and wet, never having seen a glimpse of the being who haunted her dreams.

It was unlikely, but not *impossible,* that the elemental might take offense to her overture. The fog was his home. It was, for all intents and purposes, *his* territory. By interfering with it, would she be trespassing? Possibly. Probably. But there was nothing gained in nothing risked, was there?

It didn't matter that trespassing on a predator's territory was considered a capital punishment in most of the UTA. Nor did it matter that it was not a crime that would go before jury or judge. If it came down to it, the elemental would be well within his rights to kill her without so much as a warning.

She might just end up like the scum feyrunner: left for dead on the dock because they crossed the wrong person.

"Buck up, buttercup," she muttered, raising her hands to be level with her shoulders. "You die here, at least you died chasing a story, right?"

Magic rippled out from the place all witches kept sacred, a core of solid energy that pulsed bright and hot with Glory's gifts. It lapped at her insides in a gentle hello before it surged outward, pouring through pathways that branched ever smaller and closer to the surface of her skin.

Elise breathed out, once, in a long, cleansing exhale, before she let the magic erupt from her skin in a flash.

Ordinarily, she never would have stood a chance of influencing the fog, but this close to the source, her keen inner senses snapped like a steel trap around the currents, the low hum of wild magic. Every fine hair on her body stood on end as she made contact with the behemoth swirling closer.

Magic had so many variations. It came in every color, every texture, every mood and flavor and scent and temperature and speed. It was at once all the same and so different between one pair of hands to the next that it seemed almost unrecognizable.

Elise's stomach swooped low. Like a gull diving to skim the waves just beyond her feet, it dropped into an exhilarating dive before rising, with a swift turn, to fly upward once more.

The elemental's magic — the *fog's* magic — was like clean, cold rain on her tongue. It slid against her senses with an exploratory caress. It did not buck her off like a stiff wind might, or tease her with what she could not influence like the golden rays of the sun. When she reached a hand out to it, Elise was shocked to feel it *reach back.*

"Come this way," she gently coaxed, using her affinity for manipulating water droplets in the air to slowly reel the smallest edge of the fog closer. "Come on. Just turn a little."

She didn't try to reel in the whole fog bank. Only a gloriana might be able to accomplish something like that. But even if she could have done it, Elise didn't need to. All she needed was his attention.

Which... I think I have.

It didn't take much to coax the fog, it seemed. Within a minute of contact, Elise was amazed to see the rolling, heaving clouds of the bank turn from their natural course toward the island. Normally, on a night like this the fog would have merely skimmed the jagged edges of Alcatraz.

Not tonight.

Elise dropped her arms and watched, wide-eyed, as the fog drifted over the waves to enclose the island in a white veil.

Cold licked up her arms and the exposed skin of her chest and throat. Tendrils of fog snaked around her shoes and through the wisps of hair that escaped her braid. If she thought it was quiet before, it was nothing compared to the muffled silence that pressed close to her now that she could no longer see an inch in front of her face.

Her breaths were too loud, so Elise sucked in a lungful of damp air and held it. Her muscles tensed. Her eyes flickered around her, as if she might be able to make out a shape in the impenetrable fog cocooning her.

Was he here? His fog was, but that didn't mean *he* would show his face. The fog had a magic of its own. She'd felt it and its will clearly, separate from a being of higher intelligence. Perhaps he wouldn't even notice—

A slight tug on the end of her braid made her jump.

Elise whirled around, her heart lodged in her throat somewhere. The tug felt distinctly *human.* Except there was no one there. Even the old boat house had disappeared under the blanket of fog. There was no chance she could make out a figure who stood even six inches away from her.

Trepidation tickled the back of her mind, souring the thrill of the hunt, the discovery. She really *couldn't* see anything. Even when she stretched out her senses, Elise couldn't pick up anything beyond the background roar of magic that filled the air around her.

"Hello?" she called, inanely. Was he there with her? Had her audaciously simple plan actually worked? Elise swept her gaze left and right as she tried to come up with something more to say than *hello.* "My name is Elise. I'm—"

Another tug, just on the very tip of her braid, had her whirling around. That *definitely* wasn't the fog.

Despite the way her heart pounded with excitement, Elise frowned. She liked teasing, but she didn't want to start off on the wrong foot. If he thought he could get away with playing tricks on her, she would never get what she came for.

"I don't scare easily, so you can stop trying," she calmly informed him. Swiping a lock of damp hair out of her eyes, she added, "You can't threaten me, either."

"Can't I?"

The voice was deep and smooth, with an unusual lilt that implied neither amusement nor annoyance, nor much of anything at all. It was soft, almost. As if he was used to speaking in the cotton wool quiet of the fog's embrace, or whispering against the shell of an unsuspecting woman's ear. Elise gasped as a prickle of more than just awareness danced across her skin.

Turning sharply on her heel, she intended to lay eyes on the source of the voice that could only be inches from her, but she didn't get that far.

The heel of her cute but mostly practical black boot slid against the mist-soaked boards of the dock. In the confusion of the fog, she'd misjudged how close she'd come to the edge. Like everything else on Alcatraz, there was no railing to keep her from falling.

Elise swore as she tipped sideways, fear clamping hard around her throat. Everyone knew not to enter the water after sundown. *Everyone.*

What goes in doesn't come out.

She couldn't see the water, nor the edge of the dock, but she fell all the same. There wasn't even time to panic, nor to consider what it would be like to be torn to shreds and turned into picked over bone as her other foot also lost its grip on the edge of the boards.

A hand clamped around her forearm. For a breathless second, Elise hung there, the toes of her boots pressed against the thinnest edge of the dock as a faceless being held her weight, suspending her between life and certain death in the inky water.

Elise blinked hard as a man materialized before her — not quite all the way, but enough. *Enough.*

The cool, dry palm and fingers wrapped securely around the bar of her forearm led her eye upward, over ropes of lean muscle and smooth, alabaster skin. A shoulder led to a neck, half concealed by a waterfall of white — silver? gray? — hair, and even further, up and up, to a face of smooth lines and eyes of deep, unbroken black. No whites. No irises. Just black.

His expression was placid when he murmured, "I suppose I don't need to threaten you, witch, when you're doing it perfectly well on your own."

Chapter Four

Cal held the woman over the water but didn't pull her back to safety.

She was smaller than him, but he guessed she was slightly above average height for a human. Her hair was blonde — a deep, dark gold that curled when water touched it. She had a strong, athletic frame and sharp features liberally sprinkled with freckles. Big eyes, perhaps dark green or brown or hazel, stared up at him from underneath a fringe of blonde-tipped lashes.

She was pretty, but if he wanted to, he could let her die.

It wouldn't take any effort to simply slacken his grip. She would plunge into the cold water of the Bay and be gone in an instant. The temperature would shock her system, keeping her immobile and triggering her reflex to suck in a lungful of salt water. As she fought off the paralysis of cold, the current would already be working to take her out to sea, where predators wouldn't hesitate to strip flesh from bone.

He'd seen it happen more times than he cared to remember. Luckily for this mad witch, he had no desire to see it happen to her, either.

Carefully, Cal used his much greater strength to pull her back onto the deck. The skin of her forearm was warm under his palm, just as her magic was. Even now, when she was no longer daring to influence *his* fog, it hummed between them like the aftershock of a lightning strike.

He ran the tip of his tongue along the backs of his teeth, tasting the ozone and power of her scent. It had a bite to it that tantalized as much as it aggravated.

When she was firmly on her feet, Cal released her to ease back into the comfort of his domain. He didn't retreat entirely, but he was sorely tempted to. No matter how many people he interacted with over the centuries, he never could get used to the prickly, exposed feeling that came with being observed. Best he get whatever this *Elise* wanted out of the way, then.

"Why did you summon me?"

Elise hurried to step away from the edge of the dock. He watched the exposed skin of her throat bob as she swallowed. A bead of moisture — mist condensed on her warm skin or sweat, he couldn't tell — traced the contour of her cheek and jaw.

"I didn't *summon* you," she argued, drawing her narrow shoulders back. She peered at him with open curiosity. He'd seen the look before and he didn't care for it.

Cal had no desire to be gawked at, least of all by a madwoman who thought she could tell *his* fog what to do.

Curling his fog in close, he lunged toward her suddenly, bringing them nearly nose to nose. He knew from past experience that humans tended to feel unsettled when he moved unexpectedly or in ways they couldn't, and he liked the idea of this composed, foolhardy woman feeling a little unsettled by him. Perhaps it would teach her a valuable lesson in caution.

Unfortunately, it didn't work. Elise stood straight and tall, her eyes locked on his. She didn't even blink when he accused, "You touched my fog. *No one* touches my fog. I can only imagine you wished to summon me, or else you wouldn't have dared. It's either that or you don't have any sense in that head of yours."

"I'm a weather witch," she calmly replied, unruffled, "and fog is weather, isn't it? There's no law that says I can't make contact with it. Besides, it's not like you *own* it."

No, there wasn't. Not that he gave a single thought to laws on the whole, of course. What did he care for laws? For social contracts? For politeness or imaginary authority? He was *weather.*

While she was right that he didn't *own* the fog, it was an extension of himself as well as his steady companion. It was the only home he had. No one got to influence it except him. Full stop.

He scowled. Circling her slowly, just to put her on edge, he said, "So you deny that you were trying to summon me? In this place?"

This place. Cal felt a familiar twinge of bitterness when he thought of the Aerie and its rookeries, its featureless rooms and its stern-faced acolytes. It was the closest thing he had to a real home, surely, but it brought him paltry comfort.

The acolytes might have taught him his letters and guided him through his first clumsy year of physical life, but they'd also feared and admonished him. They took him in not because they loved him, but because they felt it was their religious duty. He was a hard lesson dropped in their laps by Loft — punishment and teaching wrapped up into one confused, shaken man.

Cal swept his gaze over the witch, taking in her form fitting clothes and her flushed cheeks. He would bet anything that *she* had a real home. She looked like someone who came from a family, who knew love and bonds and what it was like to live. It was in the air around her as surely as her magic.

Unlike me.

He and this willful creature were separated by more than the fact that he was an elemental, born of sky and power and chaos. A vast gulf of understanding existed between them.

He hated it.

"Well, I'm not going to start off by lying. I did want to meet you. I just have a problem with the word *summon.* I wasn't trying to conjure you for some nefarious purpose." A smile quirked the corners of her lips upward. Cal dropped his gaze to examine that little smile. The witch had lovely, full lips but a sardonic expression that turned what might have been a sweet face into something... more. Something clever and arresting.

When he lifted his eyes back to hers, he found her watching him with a peculiar expression, as if she didn't quite know what to make of him.

He knew exactly what to make of her, though. He knew what she was and what she was after. Not even that compelling little smile could blind him enough to miss it.

Anger simmered under his skin. The fog, always attuned his emotions, rolled in agitated waves over the water.

"I see," he murmured, pushing his half-corporeal form into her space once more. Up close, he could make out every individual eyelash and sun-made freckle. He could even smell her. Below the familiar scent of brine and water, she smelled clean and fresh, like soap and flowers — exactly how he imagined a loving home would smell.

Elise blinked, but otherwise didn't react as he hovered nearer still, drawn in by the desire to unsettle her and something else he couldn't name. Perhaps it was the way her magic radiated through him, familiar and yet pleasantly foreign. Perhaps it was the warmth of her skin he could feel filling the spare inches separating them. Perhaps it was the way her tiny, nearly imperceptible gasp made the muscles of his abdomen clench.

Cal didn't know what it was that pulled him closer. He didn't care.

"You are just like the others, then," he snapped. Or rather, as close as he ever came to snapping. He spoke so infrequently that his default tone was mild, almost whispery. Even so, his displeasure came through loud and clear.

Elise blinked twice. "What?"

"You say you don't have a purpose, but you do." Cal lifted a hand to flick a damp lock of hair away from her eyes just to show her he could and would do whatever he liked. She gasped again. This time her cheeks flushed a deep, dark red. It pleased him to see it, though he didn't understand why. "See?" he accused, suddenly unreasonably angry with her. "It's in your eyes. The way you look at me. You want something."

He so rarely got truly angry, but this witch made everything in him bristle. He didn't want her to be like the others, he realized. He didn't want her to only speak to him because she wanted him to spy on someone, or kill someone, or trade something for the knowledge only he had.

Elise was pretty and he liked her smile. She smelled like comfort and her magic sang a song that made his entire being sit up and take notice.

All of that made her clear desire to use him more galling than usual.

He never hurt another being, no matter what the public thought he did. When he encountered the scum of Burden's Earth, he preferred to drop them on Patrol's stoop rather than let another stain bleed onto his soul.

But Elise didn't know that.

Surging almost out of the fog, until all but his lower legs were visible to her, Cal closed his fingers around her throat and pulled her closer, closer, until their noses brushed.

"What is it you want from me?" he rasped, staring into her wide eyes. The witch was not so composed when he had his fingers curled around her neck. He could feel the warmth of her breath ghosting over his lips, sending a bolt of some hot, hungry feeling through the brewing rage in his gut. "Are you looking for an assassin? An informant? Perhaps a spy?"

Her pulse was a thundering beat under his palm, but he had to give her credit. Elise the weather witch didn't panic. She didn't fight him. Her hands came up to stop her fall into his chest, her palms two hot brands on his naked skin, but she didn't claw or kick or shout for help.

She met his gaze squarely, without fear, when she answered, "None of the above."

Cal felt a jolt move through every fiber of his being when her fingers spread ever-so-slightly over his ribs. It was a twitch, barely anything at all, and yet he could have sworn he felt the whorls of her fingerprints moving over his skin.

His breath quickened. The pad of his thumb moved before he thought it through, pressing just under the corner of her jaw, where he was treated to the rhythmic pounding of her pulse. Each beat reverberated through him, bigger and louder than the last.

Like the familiar cadence of lapping waves, her heartbeat made a home for itself where it didn't belong: under *his* skin.

Cal's hand was much larger than her throat. Everything about him was much larger than her, despite her athletic build and long legs. When he held her this close, his hand engulfing her vulnerable neck and her face turned up to peer at him through thick lashes, she looked very fragile.

He was surprised by the way the sight, the feeling of her relaxing into what *should* have been a threatening hold, made his blood run hot in his veins. Cal wanted to shy away from the foreign feeling at the same time that he yearned to clasp it in his hands and crush it close, to keep it with him always. It was terribly heady.

A rush, he thought. Just like that time Kaz convinced him to drink one of his dark liquors, Cal felt the foreign thrill bleed into his bloodstream and cloud his thoughts, the righteous anger siphoned away to make room for something else.

"Then what are you?" he breathed, only succeeding in hiding the tremor in his voice at the last possible moment.

He saw the thoughts flashing in her eyes — what *color* were they? Why did it matter so much that he know? — seconds before he felt her fingers drag slowly down his stomach to fall away. He felt the touch all the way down to his incorporeal toes.

Her shoulders relaxed as she leaned into his hold: a sign of surrender or complete confidence?

"My name is Elise Sasini," she told him. She paused briefly, eyes flicking back and forth as if she expected some recognition he couldn't offer. Her posture was easy, submissive even, but her expression wasn't cowed. She looked at him with a confidence that raised his hackles — like *she* was the one in control. "I am a writer. I came here to talk to you. That's it."

Cal narrowed his eyes. "You're a reporter?"

She tried to shake her head, but when he tightened his grip just enough to send a message to hold still, she stopped. "No. I used to be a journalist, but now I mostly write books. Histories. Non-fiction."

Suspicion niggled at him. "What story do I have that a writer might want?"

He watched, transfixed, as Elise's expression transformed. Gone was the easy confidence. In its place, she *glowed.* Her eyes gleamed with unconcealed pleasure and that ever-present smile widened until he could see a hint of white teeth. "You have *all* of them," she explained, leaning forward unconsciously.

Cal found himself easing backward. Now *he* was the unsettled one, and yet he still had his hand wrapped around her throat. He still had the power. Didn't he?

How in the world did she manage to make him feel like she was the dangerous one?

"So you are looking for information." He tried to infuse the right amount of disgust in his voice, but he fell woefully short of his goal.

"Not like you're thinking, no." Elise lifted her arms, palms up and fingers spread, in a movement that encompassed the cocoon of fog that concealed them from the world. "I want to write about *you.* This!"

He felt her heartbeat speed up under his thumb, his own quickening to match hers, before he released her abruptly. Shock crumpled what little remained of his composure.

It was not fear that made her heart race. It was *excitement.*

Just what kind of woman was he dealing with? Realizing that

he had dreadfully miscalculated, Cal took a hasty step backward. Luckily for him, his natural grace and only partially corporeal form made the movement seem like an easy glide into the mist rather than the clumsy retreat it really was.

"Why would you want to write about me?" He shook his head. His long hair, bone white and with a will of its own, slid over his naked shoulder to wave like a flag between them. "I'm no one."

Some of Elise's radiant enthusiasm dimmed. Her brows snapped down into a harsh angle. "What? No one? You're... you're *him.* The fog! That's hardly *no one.*"

She stepped forward, completely heedless of the fact that they were invisible to the outside world, that she stood on a rickety old dock over deadly water, and that her only company was a man of untold power she didn't know.

In the years since his birth, Cal had seen every manner of depravity and form of violence. Watching over the city he once destroyed, the descendants of all those he so ruthlessly slaughtered, was his penance. It was his vigil.

He knew what could happen to a woman who stepped into a shadowed corner with a man she didn't know. He knew what happened when someone fell into the water. He knew the danger that writhed in every shadow and under every stone. He knew it all and more than he ever wished to.

Cal was suddenly vexed by her lack of caution. He was also infuriatingly charmed by it.

"You dared to touch *my* fog for this?" He gestured sharply at nothing, too agitated to much else. "What if I'd been territorial? What if I'd seen you as a threat? What if you'd slipped and *actually* fell into the water? My story can't possibly be worth what would have happened to you if I wasn't what I am."

"And what are you?"

That drew him up short. It was on the tip of his tongue to say he was a good man, one who would never actually hurt her or anyone else if he could help it, but that wasn't true. He wasn't good. He'd never had the chance to be. No one born into so much misery and bloodshed could be good.

Instead of saying any of that, Cal huffed and answered, "Someone who doesn't hurt foolish witches."

Elise's smile widened into a full grin. The power of that smile was beyond reckoning. Cal held his breath, afraid that if he moved a single muscle, that pressure building inside of him would burst, leaving him nothing but shards around her feet.

No one, not even those lucky people he rescued in all his long, long years, had looked at him like that.

"See? There was no harm in it." Her eyes twinkled with humor, like she knew how foolish she'd been and actually found it *funny.*

Cal blinked, dazed. Had he thought her pretty? Maybe he was the foolish one.

When Elise Sasini smiled at him like she kept all the secrets of the universe in her hands and found them all dreadfully silly, it made him feel the same way he did when he drifted with the fog bank over the water — weightless, exhilarated, *free.*

Like I'm home.

"No harm," he repeated numbly. "I think... there could be a great deal of harm, witch."

Not to her. She wore her confidence like armor. Maybe it really did protect her from the evils of the world. But *him...*

Cal got the uneasy feeling that if he followed the path she laid before him, he would not come out the other side the same. This woman was a force of nature all her own. Whether that was a good thing or not, he had no way of knowing. Would he like the man found on the end of the journey she promised?

Well, I can't really dislike the one I am now more, *can I?*

"What is your proposal?" he found himself asking, against his better judgment.

Elise lost her smile, but he didn't mourn it. Instead, he found himself admiring the way she pressed her lips together tightly, as if she was forcefully reining in her enthusiasm. He felt the unsettling impulse to press his fingertips against her lips, just to feel the grin they so valiantly tried to contain.

Joy burst across her expression anyway. It was uncontainable. It was in her eyes and in her flushed cheeks and in the way she propped her hands on her hips — it bled into every line of her body, like this moment in time was the most wonderful thing she'd ever experienced. It was a separate sort of magic from the one that fizzed in the air between them, but Cal was convinced it was magic all the same.

"I want to write a book about your life. All of it. From the beginning to now. How you got to be what you are, *who* you are, and everything that you've done for this city."

Cal's stomach churned. She wanted to know all of it? Why? Surely she already knew of his savage beginning. What more was there to know? His story began and ended that day. Any chance of being more was buried with his victims.

Still, he asked, "And what would I get out of this?"

Elise let out a huge breath and rubbed her hands up and down her arms. "Well, you'd get money from the book, of course. Part of the advance and royalties."

He frowned, watching closely as she unwound the knot she'd made of her windbreaker's sleeves, which were slung around her waist. She slid the jacket up and over her bare arms. When she zipped it up, he slowly replied, "I don't need money."

She cocked her head to one side. Her braid, only long enough to reach the tops of her shoulder blades and barely contained by the elastic band at the end, rustled against the reflective fabric of her windbreaker. "Everyone needs at least a little money. Surely—"

Cal waved her comment away, his skin prickling with a pleasant sort of impatience. His mind raced.

If he said no to the money, what *could* she offer him? The possibilities were at once beyond his comprehension and deeply tantalizing. "I have plenty of money I never use," he answered, thinking of the citizen's stipend he hadn't put a dent in for over a hundred years. "What else can you tempt me with?"

Elise peered at him, her brows furrowed. He kept his focus on her face, afraid to breathe, but he didn't need to look down to know her fingers moved absently through the fog caressing her hip. He *felt* it.

A shot of pure heat coursed through that simple connection. Her magic, unconscious and benign, meshed with his in an intoxicating blend. Electricity like he'd never felt leapt from her to him in a playful, erotic introduction.

It was with great surprise that Cal realized he was actually *aroused.* That had never happened before.

"What do you want?" she asked, completely unaware that her mere presence, the barest brush of her fingers, knocked his world off its axis.

Cal swallowed. It was as easy as a thought to bring the fog in thicker around him, hiding any evidence of his desire from her. He spent more than half his life in his skin, so it wasn't that he was ashamed of his nudity. Rather, he wanted to sit with this eye-opening revelation for a while before he—

What? What will I do? Tell her about how she makes my cock hard?

Maybe. He wasn't sure how something like this — his visceral attraction — was handled. Cal had never experienced its like before. His time in the Aerie and his subsequent imprisonment hadn't exactly encouraged sexual exploration, and since he'd never felt desire before this surreal moment, he had always just assumed it was part of his nature to feel no procreative impulse.

But *now...*

Now he looked at Elise and felt like a whole world had opened up to him. A gnawing hunger grew in the pit of his stomach. He wanted her to smile at him again. He wanted to feel the rush of it, the weightlessness of it. He wanted to know what it felt like to feel more than the fleeting touch of her fingers on his skin. He wanted to ease the ache in his cock and know what her kiss felt like and breathe her in with every inhale.

He simply *wanted.*

That wanting disturbed him. More than the idea that she wanted to *know* him as no other being in the world did. More than her audacity. More than the thought of her digging up all the graves he carried in his pockmarked soul.

Cal wasn't used to wanting. He didn't care for it. Certainly, wanting and yearning had never helped him before. It only caused more pain. Better to accept the ache of loneliness than to make it worse with the never-ending hunger of *hope.*

And yet, he was a curious being by nature. If there was one benefit to his vigil, it was that he got to observe and satisfy his inquisitiveness whenever it suited him. Here, now, Elise was giving him a chance to chase this new interest in an unprecedented way. Would he ever get this chance again? Would he even want it if it came?

He didn't know, and because he didn't know, Cal chose not to answer her. Not yet, anyway. "I will think on what I want," he promised her, "and give you my answer tomorrow."

"Good! Fine. That's— that's great!" Elise balled her hands into fists by her thighs, her grin surging back onto her face like an electric bolt of pure joy. "I'll be here."

Cal tried not to look at her smile, fearing what he might say and do if he let it blind him. Nodding once, he began to make his escape by way of fading into the fog, but was stopped when she made a sound of distress.

"Wait, wait!"

He paused, eyeing her suspiciously. "Yes?"

"I..." She stepped closer, her movement sending eddies through the fog clinging like a lover to her legs, hips, and sides. He shuddered at the feeling. Did she know that he and the fog had a symbiotic link? That he could feel, in a secondhand sort of way, the shape of her? No, he didn't think so, and he wasn't about to tell her. For all that it unsettled him and made the ache in his cock worse, he liked feeling her.

Her eyes were soft, almost shy, when she said, “I didn’t get your name.”

His stomach knotted. There was a reason he didn’t give out his name. Even when the people he rescued begged, just so they knew who to thank, he refused. Only Kaz knew it, though it took a decade for the orc to earn the privilege. But for reasons he could not understand, he looked into those soft, keen eyes and felt compelled to be known.

He swallowed the lump in his throat to whisper, “Cal.”

Elise made the smallest gesture — barely a gasp, almost a jolt, all pleasure — and he felt something deep inside him give way. A staggering release of internal pressure nearly sent him reeling backward. *Gods,* he thought, *I’d do anything to hear that noise again.*

“Cal,” she breathed. Her eyes gleamed in the darkness, catching the glow of the boat house’s light through the fog. “Is that short for something? Calvin, maybe? Callum?”

Cal’s chest seized as the crack inside him expanded and filled with a desire he’d never known. Panic mingled with the overwhelming urge to step out of the fog and just *touch* her. Gods, but he wanted to know what it was like to feel the silk of her cheek or the ticklish brush of her lashes with his own tarnished hands.

He didn’t know how to handle all the *wanting* that threatened to drown him in a deluge, so he needed to make his escape. Cal wasn’t certain he’d survive another moment in her presence.

“No,” he answered, fading into the familiar obscurity of the fog at last, “it’s Calamity.”

Chapter Five

FROM THE DESK OF ELISE SASINI, AN EXCERPT FROM THE MANUSCRIPT *THE SHROUDED CITY:*

No one knows weather like a weather witch. That's what my mom told me, and what her mother told her. I come from a long line of weather witches — an unbroken chain that stretches back into the fuzzy obscurity of witch hunts and elvish rule, the wild thicket of generations past. I'm no gloriana, but I'm no slouch, either. Weathercraft is in my bones. I respect the craft as much as I respect those witches who came before me.

That doesn't make my forebears right, though.

A weather witch is an interpreter. We are translators of a language in which we can never truly claim fluency. We understand and often influence, but we don't truly know *the weather. That claim can only be held by those born into the currents and storms, those rare beings who are hammered magic and earthly power.*

Elementals.

~

THE NEXT DAY WAS MISERABLE AND INCREDIBLE IN equal measure. Despite the precipitous adrenaline drop, Elise hardly slept. The thin cot and frigid room weren't the issue. Nor was the sound of people moving across the platform outside her door, presumably night dwellers and bleary-eyed pilgrims going about their business.

It was *Cal.*

Elise felt breathless and windswept for many hours after he slipped back into vapor. Her mind raced in ever-tightening circles around one subject: *him.*

He was both everything and nothing like she imagined. He was beautiful in an ethereal way that she never could have pictured. Miles and miles of smooth alabaster skin stretched over a body of lean muscle. Long, long hair flowed in currents around his aquiline face. His eyes were nothing but spilled ink, reflecting all that they saw.

Even in the dark, the sight of him made her stomach muscles tighten with ripples of awareness. Never, in all her life, had she been so potently *aware* of another being's physicality. It was as if she was hyper aware of every movement, every twitch of his beautiful fingers and flick of his hair.

Worse than all that, Elise couldn't get the sound of his voice out of her head.

Cal was soft spoken. Even when he was furious, he didn't truly raise his voice. He spoke in a murmur — a low baritone of the softest velvet. When a man spoke as if every word was a secret to be shared between them, he held untold power over the senses.

And he told me his name, she thought, staring at her half-eaten oatmeal the next morning. Her smile refused to fade even in the face of bland, overcooked oats.

Cal. Calamity.

Instead of satisfying her curiosity, he'd only thrown fuel on the fire.

Why was he named that? Did he pick it himself, or did

someone else? Why? Elise couldn't imagine a person less suited to being called *Calamity* than the hauntingly beautiful elemental.

And then there was the question of his accusations. He expected her to seek him out for *assassination?* That meant that someone had done that in the past, and Elise was terribly curious about who and when.

All day she paced the Aerie, her thoughts spinning in circles of disbelief and dizzying joy. She still couldn't wrap her head around her success, nor that he was actually considering her offer.

Well, sort of.

He did intend to ask her for something. It might have made her nervous, but Elise was aware enough of her own flaws to realize that, no matter what he asked for, she would almost certainly agree. Short of murder, there was very little she wouldn't do to satisfy her curiosity.

But if there was something else there, layered under the curiosity and the driving need to break into the marrow of a story, Elise didn't care to examine it. She understood that she was attracted to Cal, of course, but she didn't spare it much thought. The smooth skin of his palm cupping her throat might have been the single most erotic moment of her life, but she doubted he felt the same.

Could an elemental even feel lust? Elise didn't know. Not every race did.

Not that it matters, she thought, standing in the glow of the single light of the boat house. She stared out at the choppy water and hugged her arms tightly around her middle. Anticipation was a current under her skin. Would he show? Would he demand something impossible? Would he touch her like he did before?

No, stop that. Elise shifted from foot to foot. *Even if he did feel lust, you can't just assume he would be attracted to you. He's a fucking elemental. He could be into, like, clouds or something.*

But even that thought didn't stop the swooping butterflies that filled her stomach when she watched the fog move in. When it crept over the edge of the dock, she held her breath.

Cal emerged with a rolling, floating step forward. The moon was full and the sky clear. The moonlight bleached him of what little color he had, leaving him in varying shades of silvery white. Just like the previous night, he was completely naked. Not that it mattered. The fog swirled around him such that he might have worn clown pants and she would have been none the wiser. Not that she was looking, of course.

Elise swallowed, hoping her cheeks weren't flushed with her signature cherry red blush. She wanted to make a good impression, not *ogle* him. It wasn't easy, though.

Cal's expression was pensive, but there was a determined tilt to his brows that made her heart race. "Hello," she called out, trying to rein in her instinct to grin at the sight of him. *Keep it cool, Elise.* "I'm glad you came back."

He gave her a quizzical look. Gliding closer, he replied, "I said I would return."

"Well, yes, but you might have changed your mind."

Cal's lips quirked. It wasn't a smile, but more of an endearing little tick, as if he couldn't decide whether he wanted to grin or grimace. "I don't change my mind. Once I decide to do something, I keep my word."

Elise held very still, her eyes fixed on his expression. He came to a stop close to her. Only about a foot separated them. It felt like no space at all and also like a hundred miles too far.

"Oh?" she breathed, heart leaping. "Have you made a decision about my proposal?"

"I have."

Elise waited, but when he simply stared at her rather than tell her what he wanted in exchange for his story, she licked her lips and asked, "So... what are your terms, Cal?"

He lifted one long-fingered hand to touch her lips. Barely a brush, it still sent a shock of pure heat through every single one of her nerves. "I'll tell you my story," he murmured, a look of intense concentration on his aquiline face, "if I get to be with you."

Elise's mind blanked. Surely, she'd heard him incorrectly. "I... what?"

Cal's fingers slid into the hair behind her ear. Cupping the side of her head, he bent slightly to hover his mouth over hers. She felt the brush of his lips when he said, "I spent all night and all day considering what I want. I don't want money. I don't want fame or recognition. I want to know what it's like to be like everyone else for a while. I want to know what it's like to kiss you, to live like you, to touch you."

She gasped, surprised and aroused and completely baffled. This force of nature wanted *her?* Surely not in the way he implied. "For how long?" she found herself asking, as if this was something she could possibly agree to.

She couldn't. Of course not. You didn't trade that sort of thing for a story. That was at least the tenth or twelfth rule of journalism, right?

Cal's lips ghosted over her own. Cool and smooth as polished stone, they tantalized and terrified all at once. He was quiet for a moment, thinking perhaps, before he answered, "Until you finish the book."

"And you... want *what,* exactly?" On this she needed absolute clarity.

"Everything," he murmured, a strange note of pain in his voice. "I want everything you have to give me, witch. I want to try it all. But for now, I'll settle for a kiss."

Cal's kiss, when he finally committed to it, was a chaste press of his lips against hers. There was no tongue, no teeth, no groans of pleasure. It was stark and intense in its simplicity.

It wasn't like any kiss she'd had before. It tore Elise's soul out by the root and replaced it with something new. Something bigger and fuller than anything she knew before.

It was like kissing pure, intoxicating magic.

The possibility that she might say no fled under the onslaught of the desire that roared through her. When Cal gently, so very gently, sucked her bottom lip into his mouth and let out a sound of pure, unfiltered surprise — as if he'd never kissed before, gods help her — Elise knew she was lost.

Magic sang in her veins, crowing a possessive, age old song she'd never heard before: *He's mine.*

Chapter Six

FROM THE DESK OF ELISE SASINI, A NOTE SCRIBBLED ON THE BACK OF A BODEGA RECEIPT FOR ONE MNT DEW, A THREE PACK OF MEGA FREEZE MINT GUM, AND A BAG OF JALAPEÑO CHEDDAR CHIPS:

Where does he go? Someone has to know. SF is the biggest small town in the country. Everyone knows everyone. How can he have lived here for over a century and no one knows who he is/where he goes? Must live outside of the city. Why come back, tho?

HE'D NEVER KISSED ANYONE BEFORE. HE WONDERED IF it was always so...

Much.

Was it normal to feel like he couldn't be close enough to her? Did a human man kiss someone and want more with every passing second? Cal floundered under the onslaught of conflicting desires — to be closer, to tear himself away, to search for that mysterious *more* he couldn't quite grasp.

When Elise's hands slid up his chest to curl over his bare shoulders, he shuddered. Her skin was so warm against his. So different, but tantalizing. He'd never felt more comfortable in his flesh than he did when she grounded him there, her nails scraping gently at the slopes of his muscle and bones. She stepped closer, her head tipping back to a more comfortable angle, and made a soft sound of encouragement in the back of her throat.

He let out a low *whuff* of air against her lips, astonished by the headiness of touching her.

Yes, this was a good idea, he thought, the agony of his indecision firmly cast out. *Yes. Yes.*

Cal wrestled with himself over what he wanted from her, what he was willing to give her. He wanted to turn her down. His secrets were his own. He'd given his entire life to the city as penance for his crimes. He didn't owe anyone anything more.

And yet, when he thought of her sunny smile and the pulse of her magic over his skin, he could not shake the hollow ache that settled into his soul, that great fissure she had opened up in him. Cal was not experienced, but he understood that *connection* was a rare and coveted thing. Perhaps being so alone meant he understood it all the better.

Was he willing to toss away his first chance at exploring that connection with another being just to stay exactly as he was?

No.

There was no telling how this might damage him, and he wasn't even certain she would agree to his terms, but Cal wasn't a fool. He wanted to grasp this chance at that mysterious, tantalizing *something* with both hands.

And now that he held her in his arms, pressed his lips to hers, he knew there was no way he would regret this. Even if this woman somehow managed to break him into pieces, even if she betrayed him at the first opportunity, he would not regret this experiment in intimacy.

Elise's hands drifted down to trace the contours of his arms. He felt every drag of her fingertips and every soft, rapid exhale of her breath as she pulled back enough to speak.

"I... I think you need to tell me exactly what you want out of this deal," she said, voice husky.

Cal opened his eyes to find her staring up at him. Her eyes were wide and her cheeks were a deep pink. The light of the moon glinted off of the tips of her lashes. Elise was beautiful, but Cal had seen plenty of beauty in his lifetime. What was it about her that *captivated* him?

The source of his attraction was exactly what he intended to find out. *Amongst other things.*

"I want to know what it's like to be..." Cal struggled to find the right word. Didn't the races all use different words for the same thing? All he could come up with was the word his only friend used. "Mated," he finished, nodding. "I want to know what it's like to be mated."

Elise blinked. The hot pink of her blush began to cool. "That... uh, that's a big ask, Cal."

"Why?" He frowned. Smoothing his fingers through the loose strands of her hair just because he liked the texture of it, he asked, "Why is it a big deal? Don't couples do that sort of thing all the time? Explain."

"Well, yes, but not typically as an exchange for something." Her eyes darted to the side as he skimmed his fingertips through her hair. Was she shy? Or did he make her nervous?

Elise's cheeks were flushed when she continued, "What you're saying could mean anything from *we hold hands and eat dinner together* to *you want to have sex with me whenever you want.* The first one I can do, but the second one..."

Cal shook his head, suddenly aware of the vast hole in his vocabulary. What *did* he mean? Certainly not that she should feel coerced into having sex with him. He could theoretically get that anywhere and from anyone. That wasn't what he meant. Unfortunately, he lacked the experience to really articulate what he *did* mean.

Frustrated, he tried to explain, "No, I don't want that. I want... I want to know what it's like to have *everything.*"

Elise's brow wrinkled. "You said that before. *Everything.* What does that mean?"

"I don't know," he admitted. Cal blew out a breath and forced himself a few steps away from her. Being too close made an already confusing series of impulses that much worse. "I want to know what it's like to not just be *this.* I want to have a life like yours. Like everyone else. I want to know how it feels to live like you do, to have a person to *be* with. Just to see what it's like."

"You want to experience a *relationship,"* she replied, expression clearing. Elise propped her hands on her hips. "Okay. I think I know what you're asking for."

"Do you?" He narrowed his eyes at her. Cal barely understood what he struggled to put into words. How could she figure it out so quickly?

"Yes, I think I do." Elise peered at him, her expression thoughtful. "How about this: For however long it takes to write the book, you and I can be... we can explore what people in a relationship do. We can have dinner. Spend time together. If you want to know what it's like to be in a couple, we can do couple things. How does that sound?"

Cal considered her proposal for several long moments before he shook his head. "No."

"No?"

"No, I don't just want to see you occasionally," he confirmed, suddenly certain he didn't want to let Elise out of his sight. Who knew what would happen? She could decide he wasn't worth the trouble, or slip away as soon as she had what she wanted. He couldn't allow that. He *wouldn't.* "I want to know what it's like to be with someone all the time," he insisted. "I've never had that."

"You've never lived with someone else?" A curious look of sympathy settled on her features. "Do you have a home, Cal?"

It was his turn to be confused. "Yes, the fog." He gestured over his shoulder, to the rolling waves and distant, twinkling skyline. "I drift."

The closest he'd ever come to having a *physical* home was the Aerie, but even he knew it barely counted. The acolytes kept him in isolation for the first year after his creation, only allowing him companionship when it was intended to indoctrinate him into their cult. In the second year, the elves discovered his presence in their city and took custody of him. He wouldn't say the cell block beneath the Tower was his home either. Considering he escaped their dungeon and spent the next one hundred and thirty-seven years dodging Thaddeus II's increasingly aggressive attempts to recapture him, he doubted she would count it, either.

Looking at Elise's tightening expression, Cal decided to withhold those stories for now. He didn't want her pity, after all. He wanted *more* from her. Much more.

"Right, okay." She cleared her throat. Elise was quiet for a moment, her eyes pinned to some spot in the middle distance, before she appeared to come to some decision. Chin lifting, she asked, "So... why don't you come home with me, then?"

Cal was moving before he'd made the conscious decision to do so. In a moment, he was before her again, his fingers seeking out the wispy ends of her hair. He couldn't seem to keep his hands off of it. Did it only curl in the moist air, or did she wake up with a head full of curls each morning? Cal wasn't sure why it mattered to him — why all the little details that made up Elise *mattered* — but it did.

"You would take me into your home?" he pressed, incredulous, as he scanned her face for any hint of unease or guile. Surely he couldn't be that lucky. "I've never been in a real home before."

He didn't think to censor himself, but watching her expression pinch with sympathy reminded him that he probably should. Cal would give her his grim story, but he didn't want her to look at him like he was some broken thing. He wanted her to look at him like...

Well, he didn't know what he wanted, but he knew he *didn't* want that.

"I don't need a home," he felt compelled to add, for his pride's sake. "I live in the fog. I usually have everything I need, but when I don't, I come here and get whatever it is from the acolytes. What they can't give me, I seek elsewhere."

And if something was truly beyond his reach, he wasn't above trading favors with Kaz, who seemed to have his green fingers in every shady part of the city. That was how Cal ended up with so many caches, hidden behind rocks or high on unscalable cliffs or in alcoves between massive bridge supports.

Kaz was happy to provide him with whatever he asked for, but that didn't surprise Cal. The orcish spymaster belonged to the Solbournes after all, and even though he liked Kaz, he also knew that getting on his good side was all a part of the long game he and the Solbournes had been playing for over a century.

They would never get his loyalty, but he could give them a favor or two when it benefitted him to do so.

Elise bit her lip hard enough to make the rosy flesh turn white before she released it again. "But you've never had a *home,* Cal. A place where you feel safe and warm and loved."

It wasn't a question, so Cal didn't feel obligated to answer it. Instead, he soothed some of his agitation by playing with the ends of her hair. The texture was different from his. While his hair always felt thin and silky enough to be difficult to hold onto, hers was thicker, with a slight curl that continued to fascinate him.

"If I go home with you, will I feel those things?" He looked up from where he'd curled a lock of her hair around his fingertip to fixate on her lips again. They were a lovely peach color and ever-so-slightly glossy. Would she let him kiss her a second time? He felt like he'd missed something the first time and he desperately wanted to find out what it was.

Elise touched his arm. It was the lightest brush of her fingers, but it ran through him like a lightning bolt. "I don't know that I can promise that, but there's no harm in trying, right?"

Cal sucked in a sharp breath. He didn't know much about *relationships* or what it was like to have a home, but he knew there could be a great deal of harm in what they planned to do. Not to her — never to her, if he could help it — but definitely to him.

Too bad he didn't care.

Cal was hungry for the warmth she spoke of so reverently. He wanted to taste the life she lived, to bask in her smile and eat at her table and get even the briefest glimpse of what Kaz called *matehood.* He wanted all of it with a desperation that had transformed into an endless, cavernous ache, and he damn well intended to get it.

Bringing a lock of her hair to his lips, Cal murmured against the strands, "Deal."

Chapter Seven

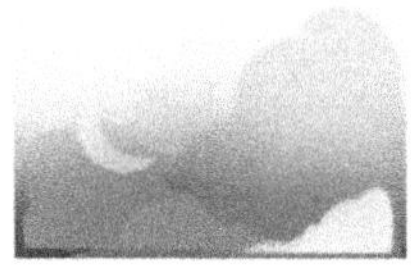

FROM THE DESK OF ELISE SASINI, TEXT MESSAGES RECEIVED ON FEBRUARY 3rd 2045:

DAD - 10:08 AM: Tell Dorothy to kiss my ass

DAD - 10:09 AM: Proud of you, kid. Keep making trouble

DAD - 10:10 AM: You should stop writing books, though. I don't need this kind of competition ;D

When she dared to imagine what it would be like to sit down with the elemental, Elise always pictured it would be in a public place. A secluded corner of Golden Gate Park, perhaps, or on the jagged rip-rap that edged the Bay, where selkies basked and foam bubbled against the shore. Their meetings would be clandestine, but in the neutral territory of a public space.

Never, in all her planning and daydreaming, did she imagine he would follow her home.

When Cal told her he would meet her on the mainland early the next morning, she didn't know what to expect. Not that she knew what to expect from *any* of this, of course. After all, who could have imagined the bargain he'd strike?

And what a bargain it was: Cal wanted to know what life was like for regular people, so for the time it took her to write his story, he would live with her, eat with her, and...

Be with her. Whatever that meant.

By the time she stepped off of the ferry and onto the early morning bustle of Fisherman's Wharf, Elise had a kink in her neck from two nights spent in the sparse conditions of the Aerie and a stomach full of butterflies.

Why exactly had she agreed to his terms? Why did she feel this gnawing, possessive feeling in her gut? What if it turned out he couldn't stand her and abandoned the deal after a night? Would he appear out of thin air? Would the fog roll in despite the bright, clear February morning, heralding his arrival?

The answer, at least to the last question, was no.

Elise adjusted her baseball cap to fight the glare of the sun bouncing off of the slate gray water. Maneuvering her way around throngs of tourists *oo*-ing and *ah*-ing over the old decommissioned warship the *EVP Shadowbreaker* docked by an overpriced seafood shack selling lobster rolls, she peeked over her shoulder at the lapping waves. He said he would meet her on the dock, but—

A hand closed over hers. The fingers were cool and smooth, the grip firm but not aggressive. Elise jumped, her head swiveling to her right.

It took her a moment to recognize him. Cal stood in the shadow between two salt crusted buildings. His face was unmistakable, but dressed in dark jeans and long-sleeved black shirt, he could have blended in with any crowd in the city. Only his long silvery hair and black eyes might have drawn scrutiny.

"Oh," she breathed, letting him slowly reel her into his shadowed alcove. Her legs felt curiously unsteady. That possessive feeling grew with a lurch, digging into her with a ruthlessness that took her breath away. Her magic fizzed in her veins. *This one is mine,* it seemed to whisper. *Don't let him go.*

Swallowing hard, she choked out, "You look..."

Cal quirked a brow and waited for her to finish her sentence, but Elise didn't have the right words to do so. Not any ones that were appropriate, at least. He looked *good.* Not in the devastating, force of nature way he looked when he melted, buck naked, out of the fog, but in the '*I could be in entertainment feeds or the face of a perfume house if I wanted'* kind of way.

Elise cleared her throat and tried again. She could feel her signature vivid blush already rising to her cheeks. "I'm sorry, I just didn't expect you to wear clothes."

Embarrassment made her cheeks flush an even deeper, darker red almost as soon as the words were out of her mouth. *Gods,* why *did I just say that?*

"Nudity draws attention." Cal's lips thinned as he glanced at the tourists shuffling across the dock. If he noticed her embarrassment, he didn't seem to care. "I don't like attention, so I've learned to stash clothing in places I can easily access."

"Right. Makes sense," she replied, vividly recalling all the beautiful, almost opalescent skin she'd been lucky enough to see. Of course it would draw attention. Any person with a functioning brain stem would notice Cal, naked or not. Close behind the memory of all that beautiful, naked skin came their kiss, which she still felt all the way to her toes.

Seeing him there in the shadow of the alley, feeling his hand holding hers, she got a dizzying sense of vertigo. Was she really doing this? Trading her companionship for a story? Was she really taking *the* fog home with her? What would her father say if he knew?

As a father, he wouldn't like it. As a journalist... Well, Bob Sasini had done a number of unscrupulous things in his lifetime to get the scoop. Surely playing house with a man for a few months wasn't worse than going undercover as a feyrunner, or becoming a temporary anchor for a crooked vampire clan.

Right?

At any rate, she knew what she was doing. And even if she

didn't, Elise wasn't certain she could just let Cal waltz back out of her life and into the fog, never to be seen again. Their meeting had altered something fundamental in her, though she still couldn't — or wouldn't — figure out what it was.

Cal's gaze slid over her flustered expression. Brow crinkling, he asked, "Is the clothing wrong? My friend chose them for me. I assumed he knew what he was doing." He frowned down at his shirt. "I did not consider the fact that he might have played a prank on me. He does that sometimes."

"No, no, you look great!" Elise waved a hand in front of her face. "I was just surprised, that's all. Your friend did a good job." Hoping to steer the conversation in a less embarrassing direction, she asked, "Do you have a lot of friends?"

Cal's expression gave nothing away. "No. Just one."

Elise didn't do what she did for a living and *not* know when someone didn't want to talk, so she let the subject drop. She made a mental note to follow up on the conversation later. "Right, well, if we want to beat the early lunch rush downtown, we should probably head to my place."

He cocked his head to one side. She watched, fascinated, as his hair flowed in the opposite direction — as if it moved with a will of its own. Was it an elemental thing, or something particular to him? "How will we get there?"

"I was going to take the m-lev. Why? How do you get around the city?"

Cal lifted a hand and flicked a finger in a dismissive gesture that was not quite wave and not quite wiggle, but some strange combination of both. "I don't need transportation."

Elise leaned forward, her interest piqued. The sounds of chatter and a busker playing kettle drums faded into nothing as she pinned her entire focus on the elemental. "How do you travel? Do you have some sort of m-gate ability?"

"M-gate?" He looked vaguely disgusted. "No, I dematerialize and ride the air currents to my destination."

Fascinating. He didn't have to travel *with* the fog to move unseen. It explained a lot of the sightings, and how he was sometimes said to appear out of thin air. She'd have to remember to put that in her notes.

"Can you take passengers?"

He shook his head. "No. Unless you can become incorporeal, you would just fall through my arms."

Elise colored as she pictured herself cradled in his arms, sweeping through the fog banks over the water at night. Butterflies fluttered low in her stomach. Of course, that sort of thing only happened in feeds, but even practical, driven Elise could indulge in a fantasy every now and again.

Shaking herself, she replied, "Well, since you can't take me with you and you don't know where I live, you'll just have to take the train with me."

She gave him her usual sunny smile to cover her nerves. Taking a step out of the shadows, she was surprised to find he still held her hand. Looking pointedly at where they were connected, she said, "Ah, you can let go. I promise I won't lose you in the crowd."

"Why?" He stepped close behind her. Cal's expression was aloof, but she didn't miss the way he scanned the crowd, nor how tense his shoulders became when a family with several young children in *Ripley's Believe It or Not!* museum t-shirts squeezed past them. One little boy clutched a colorful sparrow-shaped kite in a chubby, clawed hand.

"Oh, it's just—"

Cal nudged her forward, toward the entrance of the wharf and the m-lev station across the street. His fingers tightened around hers as his aquiline features hardened into a mulish expression. "I watch people holding hands all the time. I want to do it." He lifted his chin, adding, "It's part of my terms."

Elise swallowed. He hadn't told her much the previous night, but she didn't have to be a reporter to see the context hovering around his bargain. No one who wanted to *try* living a normal life had ever truly *had* one. Until that moment, she hadn't quite grasped what that meant.

Has no one ever held his hand before?

"Okay," she replied, smoothing out her expression so he wouldn't see her dismay. "We need to go to the other side of the street and take the outbound train."

Cal eyed the stop across the street, his brow furrowed. She wondered if he'd ever been on an m-lev before, but that question was quickly answered when she had to help him board. Elise didn't blame him for his trepidation. Although San Francisco's public transportation was top of the line, running on a combination of super charged magnets and a constantly monitored m-grid, the speed at which they traversed the hilly terrain and packed streets unsettled even seasoned riders.

However, like most public services in the EVP, it was blessedly free, so no one complained too much.

The ride took thirty minutes and was mostly fine. Cal sat beside her silently, his black eyes sweeping over the other passengers every few seconds like he thought they might whip out weapons when he wasn't looking. He never let go of her hand.

The only part that truly seemed to unsettle him was the ride through the inky darkness beneath Twin Peaks. The tunnel was only a little over two miles long and notorious for the secret alcoves and underground passageways that fed directly into the Markets up above, though the EVP government routinely sent Patrol out on sweeps to close off the illegal tunnels.

Elise was used to the stretch of pure blackness at the end of her rides home, but Cal wasn't. As soon as their car dipped smoothly underground, his fingers clenched around hers, his entire body vibrating with tension.

"It's okay. It's just a tunnel," she whispered, taking in his suddenly rigid profile. His hair, which had previously only swirled with a gentle current against his back, began to whip around them, drawing the curious eyes of their fellow passengers.

Cal turned his head to stare down at her. His expression was as aloof as it always was, except for the marked tightness around his eyes and mouth. "I don't like being underground," he explained, barely audible over the low rumble of the m-lev.

Elise wanted to pinch herself. Of course an elemental wouldn't enjoy being underground. She couldn't imagine how unnatural that would feel to someone literally made from the *sky.*

Squeezing his hand, she soothed, "It's almost over. We get off at the next stop, and then we walk up a hill. No more tunnels."

Cal nodded, but his grip on her hand didn't loosen until they were exiting the brick-lined station and stepping into the sunlight. It wasn't a quick walk back to her place, but Elise didn't mind. The trek up the steep hill to her new apartment gave her time to think.

Bringing Cal home with her was a risk. There was no telling what he was capable of. Being a weather witch meant she had some small ability to protect herself, but against a force of nature like Cal? Elise wouldn't stand a chance.

But what was the worth in uncovering a story without an element of risk? She'd made a deal, and she intended to keep it. Getting the truth about what exactly Cal did for the city and *why* would be worth it.

At the very least, it was a good excuse to keep him close.

By the time they got to her floor, Elise was flushed with exertion and giddy with nerves. Would he like her home? Did it matter? What was she going to do with him once he was settled? She'd promised him something totally amorphous. Just how far was she willing to go to give him the experience he wanted?

If she could stop thinking about his eager but infuriatingly chaste, world-shattering kiss, she might actually be able to dig up an answer or two.

Unlocking her door with an old fashioned key and a slightly out of date thumbprint scanner, she sucked in a deep breath and stepped inside.

As soon as she crossed the threshold, a pleasant, androgynous voice called out, *"Welcome home, Elise. Would you like me to turn the lights on?"*

Cal's hands closed over her hips and drew her backward into his chest. Elise let out a squeak on impact. His voice was a low bark when he demanded, "What was that? Who's in your home?"

"No one!" She wiggled to get out of his grasp, but it was no use. Cal's grip was immovable as he carefully leaned around her, his head angled to see past her entryway and into the kitchen and small living room beyond. She felt the cool brush of his magic ghosting up her spine, its tenor more aggressive than she'd felt so far.

"It's just my Met," she explained, embarrassingly breathless. "I keep weird hours, so it helps me keep track of everything. I can turn the voice activation off if it'll make you more comfortable."

"There's no one in there?"

"No, just a little rubber ball thing that knows too much about me."

Cal made a soft rumbling sound in his chest. It vibrated up her spine as he slowly eased them inside. Elise was hyper-aware of every bit of him that pressed against her back, as well as the hands that were curled over the bows of her hip bones like they were made to fit there. Magic licked over her nerves, raw and deliciously cool.

When he marched them into the space between the kitchen and the living room, she cleared her throat and pointed to the feed screen mounted on her wall. Just below it, on a small wooden cabinet, her Met sat waiting for instructions. A dull glow pulsed in its center.

"See that? It's my Met."

Cal's fingers flexed on her hips. "I don't know what that is."

Gods, just how feral is this man?

It boggled her mind to think that someone born in 1906 didn't know what a *Met* was. Surely, even if he'd never lived in a home, he'd been *inside* places before? He had to know at least some modern technology. He had to understand things like lights and showers and microwaves. If he could put on a pair of jeans, he had to know how to use a toilet, right?

Giving his hands a brisk pat as a signal to let her go, Elise explained, "It's just an extension of the internet. It's a fun bit of m-tech that can do things like manage my schedule, do basic cleaning, and set perimeter wards. Tons of people have them in their homes, Cal."

Cal slowly released her and took a step back. Turning, she watched him scan her half-unpacked apartment with narrowed eyes. "You're a witch. Why don't you set your own perimeter wards?"

Setting her bag down by the couch, she answered, "I do, but it's a convenience thing. Not all of us have the time to refresh wards every week. When I get busy, the Met does it for me."

When Cal only made that same low rumbling sound in response, Elise shrugged. "Right, well, this is my place." She waved a hand at the stacks of half unpacked boxes littering the floor. "Please excuse the boxes. I moved in last week, so I haven't had much of a chance to unpack yet. I didn't think I'd have a guest coming home with me when I left for the Aerie, or else I probably would have done more."

Or not. Elise wasn't the neatest of people. She didn't have time for all that fussing when she had words to write, stories to unspool, hidden worlds to examine. In fact, she was pretty sure some of the boxes hadn't even been unpacked in her *old* place.

Cal prowled past her, his hair moving in slow eddies around his shoulders and back. He didn't move like a man his size should. He glided across the floor and around the boxes in his way almost like he was *floating* past them. Not one of his steps made a sound.

She watched him move to the wide window that took up most of the wall opposite her feed screen. The view wasn't perfect, since the sunshine had a tendency to dredge up smog that obscured a bit of the city, but it was still gorgeous.

"You're new to the city?" Cal glanced at her over his shoulder. He looked just as intimidating silhouetted against the window as he did on the dock, though it was in a different way. Then, he hit her like a wild force of nature. Now, dressed in his black clothing and with the hard plains of his body standing out starkly against the view, he looked *dangerous.*

Elise's stomach swooped. Gods, but she wanted to unravel all of this mysterious man's secrets. Like the very first time she basked in a storm, Elise wanted nothing more than to get closer to that magnetic force, the danger he represented, and take him into the hot, burning core of magic inside her.

It was a raw sort of feeling that welled up in her from the same part of her that chased stories and scaled dangerous heights and turned her face up to feel the howling storm lash her cheeks. It was a *craving.*

"Elise?"

"Sorry!" She turned on her heel, hoping to cover up the way her blush had spread to her chest and how quick her breathing had become. Their arrangement was complicated enough. They didn't need to add her lust for thrills into things.

Swallowing her embarrassment, she waved over her shoulder, asking him to follow her as she escorted him to her office-and-guest-room. "To answer your question, no, I'm not new. I was born and raised here. I just moved into this place because it was better than my old apartment."

She couldn't hear his whispering steps moving across the floorboards as he followed her down the hall, but she could feel his nearness. "Why is it better?"

Casting him a smile over her shoulder, she answered honestly, "Because it has a better view of the fog, of course."

Chapter Eight

Homes were strange places. Cal knew that long before Elise invited him into hers, but he experienced a whole new appreciation for the concept after he stepped inside.

It had all the basics he was familiar with from his time in the Aerie and his confinement under the Tower: walls, doors, a mattress he presumed was for sleeping, and a washroom. He'd peered through enough windows in his lifetime to know that Elise had much of what everyone else seemed to have, too, such as comfortable furniture and a vast collection of baubles he couldn't quite wrap his head around.

However, there were several key differences between what he expected and what he experienced.

First, Elise's home *smelled* nice. As soon as he walked through the door — an oddity on its own, considering he had never been invited into a home before — Cal was hit by a pleasant, unnameable fragrance. A blend of her natural, crisp scent and something warmer, it made his stomach tighten with a tension he couldn't decipher. A far cry from the cold, musty smells of the Aerie and much better than the dank, chemical scent of the Solbourne dungeon.

Second, she didn't lock the doors or set wards. Elise barely even glanced at her perimeter wards. When he reluctantly stepped into the guest room she provided for him, he half expected her to slam the door and immediately throw up a ward to try and imprison him inside. Despite his eagerness, he was morbidly curious: Would she reveal a true, darker motive behind her story?

It turned out the answer was no.

Elise was sunny and cheerful as she arranged a bed for him, chattering about how she'd been lucky enough to "snag" the apartment, and how her father's book somehow played into it. He could barely follow the story, since he was too caught up in watching her move and listening to her chipper, fast-paced voice. When she was done, she didn't even close the door.

She walked out of the guest room, hips swaying in her tight black leggings, and Cal stared after her. He listened to the sounds of her moving about the half-unpacked apartment with growing perplexity.

Yes, he made the deal and intended to follow through with it, but there was a large part of him that still believed she was somehow looking to use him. Even when he stood on that crowded dock and held her hand, he wondered how long it would take for her to show her true intentions.

But Elise hadn't shown him anything other than genuine kindness. She wanted something from him, but it was nothing he couldn't afford to lose. What he stood to gain from their deal was worth far, far more than his story.

Cal sat on the edge of the fold out bed. It creaked under his weight, but he barely noticed it as he glanced around the room. The guest room held a few scattered boxes with hasty scrawl across their faces. Spiky handwriting labeled them as '*office I guess*', or '*fragile - DO NOT DROP!!*', and even the amusing '*????*'. He didn't know why that made him smile, nor why seeing it made him feel like he knew Elise a little better.

Cal's gaze wandered over the haphazard stacks of cardboard to land on her desk. A bulletin board loomed over it, so laden with pinned notes and photos that none of the cork board could be seen. The desk itself was nearly swallowed up by stacks of recycled books and scattered sticky notes. What did it say about her that she seemed to prefer old fashioned pen and paper? Cal didn't know, but he found it endearing anyway.

Eyes lingering on what looked like a photo of the fog sweeping over the ruins of the Sutro Baths, Cal focused on the sounds of Elise moving around in the kitchen. A door opened with a strange sucking sound, and then there was a smaller clatter of glass knocking against itself.

He could picture the scene perfectly in his mind. How many times had he glimpsed people in their kitchens, moving with a rhythm he didn't understand? He could imagine Elise standing over a cutting board, knife in hand, as a man slid up behind her to kiss the long line of her throat, fingertips sliding under the hem of her shirt to tickle her skin.

Cal scowled. He didn't like that image.

Fisting a handful of the blankets she'd so painstakingly laid out for him, he considered the complex question of what he wanted out of this deal and how he planned to get it. She was right that he wanted a home, but he felt in his bones that he wanted something more than that, too. Unfortunately, he didn't have the vocabulary or experience necessary to define it. A mate was the closest thing he could manage, but even that didn't feel right.

Kaz explained to him that a mate was something special. Something like a home and a lover and a best friend and a fascinating stranger all wrapped up in one being. Cal hungered for that. He just wasn't sure he was going about getting it in the right way.

Would Kaz approve of his bargain with Elise? Not that Cal *needed* the orc's approval, of course, but he was the only person he could even passingly count as a friend. He was also the only person Cal knew who understood matehood, even if he wasn't personally mated yet. Orcs held matehood sacred. Though he never understood the appeal in the past, he was beginning to get an inkling as to why so many revered the bond between mates.

What would it be like to be allowed into every corner of someone's life? Would he see himself in the home as much as he saw Elise in every note, in every breath he took? What kind of privilege was it to be let that close to another being? Cal could barely comprehend the enormity of the questions that circled his mind in agitated gusts. He'd never given himself the luxury of imagining himself in the position he now found himself in.

If he had learned anything since his disastrous birth, it was to follow his instincts. They had yet to guide him wrong, and they were currently telling him that whatever it was he *needed,* Elise had it. That impulse was clear enough, at least.

Feeling confined, as he usually did when he spent too long in his physical form, Cal stood up from the bed he probably wouldn't use and followed the sounds and smells coming from the small kitchen.

"I don't sleep," he announced, agitated and craving her attention.

Elise froze, a silver spatula poised over two identical sandwiches in a pan. A heartbeat later, the tension unwound from her shoulders. She turned her head to look at him with a baffled smile. "Oh, I didn't know that. Sorry. Don't worry about the bed, then."

Cal prowled closer. The smell of something savory drew him in, as well as the unwavering impulse to be close to her. "I rest, but I don't sleep like you do. When I dematerialize, I can do something *like* sleeping, but it's not the same."

He wasn't sure why he felt compelled to tell her this, but he did. Perhaps it was because he felt like he'd learned so much about her since he stepped into her home, or maybe it was that hungry thing in him, desperate to be known by someone, anyone. Whatever it was, the words came spilling out without his permission.

She blinked, her smile dimmed only slightly, but otherwise appeared unfazed. Did nothing ruffle her? Surely she didn't spend enough time with other elementals to take *everything* he did in stride. There weren't exactly scores of them dropping out of the sky — as far as he knew, anyway.

He didn't like how that thought made him feel, either. He wanted to be the only elemental she spent her time with. She was his mate for the time being, wasn't she? That meant he was hers. He didn't want to share her even in his imagination.

Feeling vexed and more confused than ever, Cal did the only thing that actually seemed to help his mood. He stepped up behind her and wrapped his hands around her trim, athletic waist. Coils of mist unfurled from the edges of his form to curl around her shoulders and lithe legs, anchoring them together.

That's better, he thought, releasing a harsh breath. The feeling of constriction vanished when he slid his dematerialized form over her. Magic sparked between them — her innate, stormy nature calling to his own wild energy. Together, they hummed in perfect sync.

We fit, he thought, fingers tightening around her waist.

Finally, Elise looked surprised. The spatula made a soft *ting* when she lowered it to the rim of the pan. "Cal? Are you okay?"

"I'm not used to being in this form for so long," he admitted. It was true, if not the whole reason for his agitation. "It is restricting."

"I can imagine it would be." She flipped one of the sandwiches, revealing a perfectly browned slice of bread. Cal watched her movements greedily, never having been afforded such an intimate view of a domestic task. "Does touch help?"

He eyed the way her long fingers curled around the handle of the spatula and was surprised by the vivid, erotic image that rushed to the forefront of his brain. His cock chose that moment to remind him of its crucial role in this deal of theirs. The sensation still unsettled him. Would it react like this to everyone now, or just her? Did he even *want* to feel this way for anyone else?

"I'm not sure," he answered, for more reasons than she could properly guess. "But I like touching you. I've never gotten to touch anyone before."

Elise turned her head so fast, she came very close to slamming her cheek into his shoulder. He frowned and leaned back as she said, "You've— I'm sorry, what?"

He eyed the sandwiches in the pan. They were beginning to smoke. "Are they supposed to do that?"

"Shit." She waved her hand over the induction stove's keypad. A friendly chime sounded, apparently to let everyone know that the burner had been deactivated. Carefully scooping the slightly charred sandwiches onto two waiting plates, she asked, "What do you mean you've never gotten to touch anyone before, Cal? Everyone touches people."

"I don't." He found himself giving her waist a small, possessive squeeze. "Not until now, anyway."

And what a luxury it was to touch her. Elise was warm and soft, but with a strength to her that spoke of activity, vitality. She was the kind of woman he might see jogging across the black sand beaches at sunrise, or hiking the Twin Peaks trail on a hot day, sweat glistening on her golden skin. He felt like he was holding something more tangible, more preciously human, than he had any right to be.

Guilt and shame gnawed at him, demanded he wash himself of such small, essential pleasures as touching and being touched, but Cal selfishly pushed them aside. For once, he didn't want to listen to the damning voice the acolytes had given him. He wanted to know what it was like to have a mate, and he intended to do so.

With the sandwiches settled and the stove turned off, Elise turned slowly in his arms. With her arms extended backwards, she curled her fingers around the oven door's handle, as if she needed to brace herself for what she said next. "Cal... Have you really never had any human contact before? *None?*"

Cal indulged his selfishness by skimming the pads of his fingers down the length of her arms. She was wearing a little blue t-shirt with the words *RUTH ASAWA HIGH* printed on the front. It was faded and thin, with short sleeves that revealed all the strong lines and smooth skin of her freckled arms.

"Loft's acolytes aren't exactly known for being touchy," he dryly answered. "The year I spent with them did not include hugs and kisses. The year I spent in the Solbourne dungeon didn't either."

Oh, he'd certainly had physical contact, but only the kind that came at the end of a fist, so he didn't bother counting it.

And after an introduction to the world such as that, why would he seek out companionship? The only kind he was ever offered came with deadly strings attached. Kaz didn't count. Their friendship was based mostly on a mutual exchange of information and the respect two predators had for one another. It was the closest thing to companionship he ever had, but even he knew it wasn't what he really wanted.

After a while, he stopped wondering what it would be like to be held the way he saw others hold their loved ones. To kiss. To have his hair stroked. To fuck.

Until Elise, of course.

Their arrangement had strings, but they were the kind he could tolerate. She didn't want him to commit more sins, but simply to tell his story. In exchange, he would finally know all the delights he assumed were out of his reach.

She stared up at him with wide eyes, her lips parted with surprise or horror or something else he couldn't fathom. Her fingers went white around the silver handle of the oven door. "So you've never hugged anyone? Kissed? Nothing at all?"

Cal's eyes darted back up from where they had been contemplating the delicate curve of her clavicle. At some point, she'd cut a slit in the collar of the old shirt. It sagged, just a little, and revealed her winged collar bones to his hungry gaze.

"I've kissed *you,*" he reminded her. *And I will do it again.*

Cal chose not to say the second part aloud, but the flush in her cheeks told him she picked up on it anyway.

He watched, fascinated, as Elise took in a large breath and

then slowly let it out. Her fingers uncurled from around the handle one by one. Turning slightly to the side, she picked up the plates. When her eyes met his again, they were glowing with a sort of determination he'd never seen directed his way before. It was at once breathtaking and terrifying.

Her voice was low with restrained emotion when she said, "Let's have lunch, and then... *Then* you need to start telling me your story, Cal, because I have so very many questions."

Chapter Nine

FROM THE DESK OF ELISE SASINI, A TRANSCRIPT OF A VOICE RECORDING DATED FEBRUARY 4th 2045:

CALAMITY: What do you want to know? Everyone knows my story already.

ELISE: I don't think that's true. People know the story of the disaster, and they know the legends about you, but they don't know the truth about who you are and what you do.

CALAMITY: And what makes you think those things aren't the truth?

ELISE: Maybe truth isn't the right word. I'm talking about... [PAUSE] everything else. You're more than just what happened in 1906, Cal.

CALAMITY: [LENGTHY PAUSE] That's where you're wrong.

Elise had interviewed many people in her career. She had, after all, started working as a journalist when she was ten — for her own newspaper, of course. *The St. Francis Chronicle* wasn't the most prestigious paper of record, but it kept the neighborhood abreast of all the latest developments, like when Mrs. Manfredi put an illegal pool in her backyard or that time the neighborhood association tried to exterminate the pixies in the park's shed, despite it being against the city's environmental bylaws to do so. It's reputation was helped by a ringing endorsement from San Francisco's most celebrated crime writer, Bob Sasini, who lived on 113 Santa Clara Avenue, and happened to be the publisher's amused father.

Hopping from her little paper to school journalism, then to *The Light* and her own books, Elise had more experience with interviewing than most journalists her age. She learned all the best tricks at her father's knee, and she'd honed her skills on the rolling, bouncing San Francisco streets.

None of that helped her with Cal.

No matter how hard she tried to keep things straight, to stay in the cool, professional headspace that allowed for an objective interview, she just... couldn't manage it.

Perhaps it was the memory of his kiss and the greedy, possessive hands that reached for her at every opportunity. Maybe it was the way he sat across her small kitchen table, his black on black eyes fixed to her face like he was the one trying to figure *her* out. Elise suspected it was a mix of both, as well as the fact that she struggled to stomach some of the things he told her.

Cal was stark in his honesty. He didn't sugarcoat things, and he didn't seem to understand social niceties. He was reluctant to talk about some things, but she didn't think it was because he was trying to hide anything. Elise quickly realized that, like his heartbreaking inexperience with physical contact, Cal was similarly unfamiliar with *talking* to people.

And no wonder. The more she learned about his story, the more she tried to understand why he talked to anyone at all.

"Cal..." Elise's voice trailed off into nothing, her words evaporating into so much dry air in her throat. She sat across from him, both of their grilled cheese sandwiches sitting cold and untouched on their plates, and tried to quell the urge to reach across the table to hold his hand.

That wasn't what interviewers did. They let their subject say what they needed to with a patient detachment, guiding only when absolutely necessary. She wasn't supposed to feel the prick of tears behind her eyelids when he explained, expressionless and without inflection, the circumstances of his birth to her.

"It was my fault," he continued in his soft, deadpan voice. "Every one of those deaths is on my soul. All three thousand of them."

Elise had to swallow twice before the lump in her throat shrank enough to allow her to speak. She shifted her weight in her chair. Fighting the urge to comfort him somehow, she tucked one leg under her and fisted her hands in her lap.

"Is that what the acolytes told you?" she asked, her tone brittle with outrage.

Cal inclined his head. His hair, starkly white against his black shirt and the glorious sunset streaming through the windows behind him, flowed in slow currents around his shoulders. "They took me in," he explained, "and they taught me how to be with people. I didn't understand what had happened to me for weeks afterward. I couldn't understand them, the things they said, or why my form was different than it used to be. When I finally learned their language, all they ever talked about was my sin, and how Loft had given me to them so that they could teach me how to atone for it. They thought I was a test of their devotion."

Elise knew it wasn't helpful, but words spilled out of her anyway. "But.. But Cal, it *wasn't* your fault. You didn't have any control over it. No one gets to control how or where they're born."

Cal's fingers moved restlessly over the tabletop. Although his expression didn't change, she could tell he was getting restless. His long hair had begun to dematerialize into wisps of fog, and she could feel the cool kiss of it along the skin of her arms and bare feet.

Remembering what he said about feeling confined, Elise eschewed the last of her tenuous control over her professionalism and reached across the table.

Cal's eyes widened when her fingers curled around his. For a moment, he felt strange, almost not-quite-there, and Elise realized that he had barely managed to keep his physical form as he told his story.

As soon as their skin touched, he solidified. That hungry look gleamed in his eyes as he snatched at her hand, holding it like he thought she might try to rip it away from him.

Tracing the contours of her knuckles and short, clear-coated nails with his fingertips, he said, "It doesn't matter. It's my fault, and I'll spend the rest of my life trying to make up for all the death I caused."

Elise's fingers spasmed. His naked honesty hit her like a bolt to the chest. She expected him to be mysterious, not *tortured.* "Is that why you watch over the city? Because you feel like you have to atone for 1906?"

"Yes."

Trying to make sense of the tangle he presented her with, she shifted subjects. It was much for his sake as hers. She wasn't sure how much more sorrow she could withstand before she leaned over the table to take him into her arms. "You mentioned that you were imprisoned. How does that fit in with the Aerie?"

"Much of the Aerie was destroyed in the disaster. They needed to rebuild. I wasn't locked away so much by the end of my first year, mostly because I didn't know where to go or what to do with myself. I used to stay around the dock to be closer to the fog. One day, a builder caught me rematerializing and contacted Patrol." He shrugged, but she could feel the tension in the hand that held hers. "The acolytes fought for custody of me, claiming it was their religious right, but the sovereign wanted me under his control."

Elise paled. Although it was before her time, she knew there was no arguing with Thaddeus II. Even before he lost his mind, the man was legendarily autocratic. His word was law, and if he wanted something, he used any means to get it.

"How long were you imprisoned?" she dared to ask, her dread solidifying into a sickly weight in her stomach.

Cal lifted her hand up to his mouth almost experimentally. Slowly, he pressed his lips to the center of her palm. A *zing* of magic shocked her nerve endings and sent a wave of heat through her, adding to that possessive fire in her belly. She watched his eyelids flutter, white lashes brushing the tops of high, blade-like cheekbones with a breathless sort of hunger.

His whisper tickled the sensitive skin of her palm. "Four hundred and three days."

Horror wiped away the tantalizing rush of desire in her veins.

Four hundred and three days. On top of what was a sort of de facto year of isolation in the Aerie. Over two years of confinement and indoctrination of a being meant to run as wild and powerful as the rolling fog.

The isolation and confinement alone would be enough to scar anyone, but an *elemental...* Elise shuddered to think about what that must have been like for him. And that was before she dared probe into what exactly Thaddeus II did to him during that time.

Even before he became Mad Thad, the sovereign wasn't known for his mercy. No elves were.

Elise angled her hand to cup his jaw. Cal's skin was perfectly smooth, no hint of stubble. The deep black of his eyes glittered in the orange light of the sunset as she smoothed her thumb over one beautifully cut cheekbone.

"I'm sorry," she whispered, blinking back tears. "I'm so sorry, Cal."

Gods, when she made her proposal to Dorothy, when she thought up the idea to write *The Shrouded City,* she never once considered it would end up with her sitting across her kitchen table from a man carrying so much hurt.

Cal was an almost mythic figure. He was a legend she grew up with, an all-powerful child's daydream and seductively dangerous adult fantasy.

He wasn't supposed to be... broken.

And he was broken. She could see it in the suspicious way he watched her, as if he expected her to do something to hurt him every time she opened her mouth. It was written in every gesture, every flat word and in the almost defiant way he reached for her, as if daring her to deny him this comfort he so obviously craved.

Glory save me, she thought, wracked with a sudden wave of bitter guilt. Bile crawled up the back of her throat. *I can't write this book.*

Elise withdrew her hand abruptly and stood up from her chair. She turned her back on him and tried to get her composure. Of course she'd heard tragic stories before. Of course she'd done hard, gut-wrenching interviews. This was different. Something about Cal twisted her up inside until the tension was too much too take.

There was no thrill of discovery in his story anymore. There was only a deep, painful ache in her heart.

Pressing her palm over her racing heart — the same one he kissed — Elise choked out, "I... Cal, I don't know if this is such a good idea."

His gaze sharpened. "What?"

They hadn't even gotten to the part about people always wanting to use him for something, but now she could imagine it all too clearly. Mad Thad wanted to use him, probably as security for the city, if not as part of his secret shadow arm of Patrol. No doubt others had the same idea. A person who could be anywhere he wished without being noticed, who could see and hear anything in the city, was someone to have on your side whether they actually wanted to be there or not.

Of course people would want to use him.

Just like I am.

It didn't matter that he'd agreed to it. It didn't matter that he was getting something out of it. It didn't even matter that she felt like his story still ought to be told, so he could finally see that he was more than the crushing guilt he carried. She talked a big game on that dock about not wanting to take advantage of him like he thought, but was she really so different from those who came before her?

No. She felt a deep kinship with this exquisite, broken being, and now she couldn't bear the idea of exploiting him for something as shallow as a *book.*

No contracts had been signed yet. Things were still in negotiation. There was time to back out, to say she didn't feel comfortable with the story. It wouldn't look good, but a hit to her reputation was better than this ugly feeling of guilt that ate at her insides like corrosive acid.

Turning around, Elise found Cal standing up from his seat, his brows lowered over his eyes and his mouth pressed into a hard line. One hand was flattened on the table top, while the other was a tight fist by his thigh. He looked furious. Of course he did. He probably realized just how awful she was.

Elise lifted a shaking hand to push a lock of hair out of her eyes. "Look, Cal, I'm sorry. I didn't know. If I had, I wouldn't have— I wouldn't have done any of this. I would have just left you alone. I'm sorry. I'm going to call my editor and tell her that I can't write the—"

Magic slid over her skin. In the blink of an eye, her apartment filled with a haze of cool fog. Elise gasped. The air was wet and sweet on her tongue, but she didn't have time to appreciate it.

Cal rose to his full height, his expression thunderous. His hair whipped behind him, almost entirely dematerialized into his summoned fog, and his black eyes were hardened into pitiless obsidian.

"You're going back on our deal?" he demanded, swooping toward her in one long, very *unhuman* stride. Elise backed up until her spine hit the edge of the kitchen counter, but he didn't stop his advance until he was pressed up against her. Cal's fingers gripped the edge of the granite slab, trapping her there.

Elise felt the hard press of his body along the length of hers more than she felt the edge of the counter biting into the small of her back. Magic was thick in the air between them, bright like ozone but with a sharp metallic tang like blood.

"Cal, you've been used *enough,"* she explained, voice hoarse. "I don't think I can go through with this knowing that I would just be another in a long line of people trying to exploit you."

His eyes narrowed until they were little more than glittering shards of black stone in his silvery face. "I don't care if you exploit me. I want what you promised."

Gods, and what a cruel promise it was. More guilt curdled her stomach. Thank Glory she hadn't actually touched her grilled cheese. If she had, Elise wasn't sure she would have been able to keep it down.

"I shouldn't have agreed to your terms." A flash of something very close to hurt passed over his expression. *Oh, no. I can't hurt him. I can't.* Panicked, Elise reached for him with both hands. She twisted his shirt in her fists and rushed to explain, "Cal, listen. When I agreed, I didn't realize the extent of your... of what you'd been through. I never would have agreed to it if I knew. You deserve a home and love and all the things we talked about not as a *deal,* but because it's your right as a sapient being. I can't stomach the idea of being someone who gives that to you for the first time, only to rip it away as soon as our transaction is done. You deserve better than that."

Just the idea of sending this poor soul packing the moment the book was finished made her ill. It was all fun and games when she thought he was just socially awkward or inexperienced, but this was different. What kind of monster *was* she?

Cool hands cupped the sides of her neck. Cal's grip was firm; his thumbs pressed hard into the line of her jaw. Elise stared up at him with wide eyes as he clearly struggled to find the words for something. To tell her off? To shame her for what was so clearly a terrible mistake?

"No." His voice was louder, harder, than she'd yet heard it.

This was no murmur. It was a stone cold demand. "No, I do not accept this. I want our deal. I'll have it, Elise. I *will.*"

"Cal—"

His mouth crashed down on hers. She yelped, surprised by the flash of pain caused by her lips hitting her teeth, but she didn't pull away. Cal angled her head back and leaned into her until all she could see and smell and feel was him.

The pressure on her lips softened as he molded his mouth to hers, seeking something he clearly didn't know how to find. Elise's heart lurched in her chest. She was his first kiss. One hundred and thirty-nine years old, and he had only ever kissed *her.* No wonder he felt so desperate as he slid his lips against hers, a needy sound rumbling in the back of his throat.

Cal was starving for affection. She'd callously dangled hers in front of his nose, only to snatch it out of his reach by backing out of their deal.

Elise felt something in her crumble. The last clinging remnants of any professionalism were swept away with her rejection of their deal. Perhaps he wouldn't let her back out of the deal, but that didn't mean she had to actually go through with it. If she was going to do this, it wasn't going to be a transaction. It occurred to her that he may not feel comfortable interacting with her *outside* of the structure of a deal, and that was unacceptable. She couldn't let him go.

Elise would keep up the facade of their deal, but it wasn't going to be because she wanted something from him. She wouldn't be another in a long line of *takers.*

Fierce possessiveness and the overwhelming desire to protect this incredible, damaged being swept through her, scouring her doubts like a bitter wind.

For once, Cal was going to know what it was like to *receive.*

Elise untangled her fingers from the hem of his shirt and smoothed them upward, over the trim expanse of his stomach and the sweep of his chest. Curling her arms around his back, she stroked the muscles bracketing his spine with careful slowness. He shuddered, lips stilling their frantic movement against hers. His breaths puffed in harsh exhales against her cheeks.

She hummed a soft, soothing note and leaned into him, guiding the kiss into something softer, deeper. Her lips parted and she very gently swept her tongue over his bottom lip. The noise of hungry surprise that escaped him made her stomach muscles tense. A pounding heat took up residence between her thighs.

It didn't take him long to realize what he'd been missing. Cal was a voracious kisser. He let her lead, but she got the sense that it was only because he was learning, figuring out what he liked. As soon as he realized he could *taste* her, Cal kissed her like the starved creature he was.

Elise's blood was molten with desire. The magic between them was saturated with it. Even the fog obscuring the interior of her apartment began to crackle with the neon pink and teal sparks of her energy. Every slide of his tongue against hers, every soft groan of pained pleasure he made, every unconscious rock of his hips into hers made her pulse throb with a deep, achy rhythm between her thighs. Gods, she *wanted* this man more than she'd wanted anyone in her life.

Moving her hands back around to press against his chest, Elise tore her mouth away with a ragged gasp. She had to go slow. He was new to this, and making sure he was comfortable and *ready* for intimacy was essential.

Cal made to follow her retreat, chasing her lips with his own, but she turned her head away. "Cal, we need to talk about—"

His lips, wet and swollen from her kisses, trailed over her cheekbone to press against the shell of her ear. "Don't take this from me, witch," he rasped, mistaking her protest for a rejection. "A deal is a deal."

He paused, breathing hard, before he begged in a broken whisper, "Please don't take this from me."

Elise squeezed her eyes shut. How in the gods' names could she refuse him? If it was a deal he wanted, then she would just have to give it to him — in her own way.

Chapter Ten

FROM THE DESK OF ELISE SASINI, AN EXCERPT FROM THE MANUSCRIPT *THE SHROUDED CITY:*

He calls himself Calamity.

The word is derived from the ancient Latin term 'kadamitas', meaning loss or defeat, and later, more recognizably, 'calamitas', meaning disaster, damage, or great misfortune. The word took a winding route through medieval French — 'calamité' — to finally settle in the crowded bed of fifteenth century English as 'calamity'.

When I first met Cal, I was taken aback by the implication of such a name. Of course, knowing the only clear facts about his history available to the public, I thought I knew what it referred to, but I was still surprised.

Did he name himself? If so, why would he choose a name that called back to a disaster that took the lives of over three thousand people?

Knowing him as I do now, with the intimacy and constant, pleasant surprise of a mate, I am no longer reminded of the grim events his moniker immortalizes. Like everything else in his life, Calamity was forced upon him. When I hear it, I am reminded that he is a man who has grown into his own agency, despite the world attempting to take it at every turn.

He is *Calamity. He is a force of nature more powerful and vast than our government would comfortably admit. He is all-consuming. He is an act of godly wrath made flesh, and by some miracle, he has chosen to be kind to us.*

He is Calamity. He is mine.

Over the next few weeks, they settled into life together. It was no small task, considering Cal had never lived in a home before, let alone alongside another person. Routines had to be established, habits reorganized, and questions answered. Cal learned to use the stove — though he mostly preferred the greasy takeout the rare times he actually ate — and Elise got used to his constant coming and going.

Though she'd hinted at the conversation several times, testing the waters, Cal refused to let her out of their deal, so Elise stuck to her plan.

Cal held strictly to the terms she'd foolishly agreed to, but, after a sleepless night of internal debate and recrimination, she decided that there was no harm in letting him think they were still exchanging favors if he wanted to. For her part, there was no deal to speak of.

When he drifted into the apartment after long stretches of what he called his *vigil,* Elise did the job he expected of her: she listened to him tell his story, asked questions at the appropriate times or when things needed to be clarified, and wrote. He didn't need to know that she had no plans to publish the manuscript. As far as she was concerned, it was a way to get to know him and a handy excuse to keep him near. That was all it needed to be.

The more she learned, the more certain of her feelings she became. What began as a plan to find the truth behind the man in the fog became a carefully constructed artifice covering up a campaign of warlike affection.

Cal was taciturn and abrupt. He didn't like not knowing how to navigate a situation, and some days she only saw him in snatches, or as a low-hanging mist curling around her ankles. Elise discovered that, when he felt particularly grouchy or confined, he preferred to dematerialize. She didn't mind it, though the habit had finally forced her to unpack her boxes, lest the cardboard absorb any more moisture and simply dissolve onto her floor.

He wasn't an easygoing man, but the more time they spent together, and the more of his story he laid bare before her, Elise knew she'd made the right choice. Beneath the angry, confused man was a being aching with loneliness. What began as a consuming need to know his story quickly morphed into a different kind of desire and a possessiveness that took her breath away.

Elise knew she was probably headed for heartbreak. Courting a man who didn't even realize what was happening was a disaster in the making. She had no assurances that he would not be completely happy to up and leave her as soon as he thought their exchange was complete, but she firmly pushed that thought aside.

Their time together was distraction enough. It was easy to forget about the tenuous ground they stood on when her days and nights were filled with Cal. They watched feeds together, though he was mostly bemused by them. They went on long, winding walks together, swapping stories about their lives in the city. They ate and drank together. She taught him the joys of a hot bath and he showed her gorgeous, hidden alcoves in the rough coast. They lay together in the cool, black sand under the Marin side of the Golden Gate and they danced slowly in her kitchen when a slow song came on the Met.

The look of intense concentration and amazement he wore when he stroked her skin, the sounds he made when she set aside her tablet to straddle his lap and kiss him breathless, the expression of confused delight he wore when she asked to braid his hair — all of it gave her that delicious swooping sensation in her stomach that the thrill of chasing a story gave her. Loving on Cal was a greater high than any undercover work or corruption scandal or cold case.

Elise knew she had to be careful with him. She was ever-conscious of his inexperience and of how very fragile he could be. Perhaps she was even more aware of it because he didn't seem to realize what dangers could await him if he got in too deep with an arrangement like the one he *thought* they had. Protectiveness thrummed through her every time they discovered some new, heartbreaking thing he had been deprived of.

So she handled him with the utmost delicacy and did her best to navigate the thorny brambles of his past, all the while pretending like she *needed* to write his story down.

That part was no hardship either, really. The words flowed out of her even when he wasn't lingering in her home, inspecting gadgets or curling up behind her on the couch. Cal's story was an incredible one. It was perhaps the most interesting and moving thing she'd ever heard, let alone written.

It was a shame that no one would ever see it, but Elise didn't mourn too much. Instead, she took the opportunity to step back from professionalism. She wrote not just the stories Cal relayed to her, but her impressions of him, her admiration for him, and about the cliff's edge of her feelings she could feel creeping closer every day.

It was a beautiful, raw book chronicling their time together. It was, at its heart, a love letter to Cal himself.

Chapter Eleven

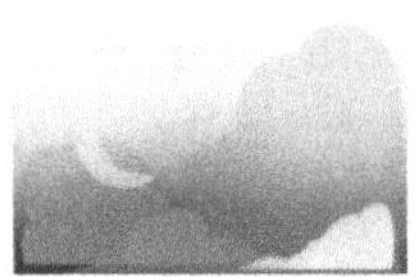

FROM THE DESK OF ELISE SASINI, TEXTS RECEIVED FEBRUARY 15th 2045:

MOM - 12:15 PM: ur coming 2 dinner tonight, right??? We haven't seen u in weeks!!! I MISS MY DAUGHTER

ELISE - 12:17 PM: Will there be cake? I demand tribute for the gift of my presence, mother

MOM - 12:17 PM: My love for u is better than cake!!!!!

ELISE - 12:18 PM: False.

MOM - 12:18 PM: I can't believe I raised u

ELISE - 12:19 PM: xoxo see you tonight! Oh, also, I'm bringing a guest. Hope that's okay byyyyyye

"I don't come here often," Cal mused. He tilted his head back to examine the huge trees looming over them. The air was spicy in this neighborhood. Almost peppery.

Elise squeezed his hand. Her voice was full of warmth when she told him, "Those are old growth eucalyptus trees. Don't they smell nice?"

"They do." Although they weren't his favorite scent. That

belonged to the woman strolling next to him, her golden hair shining in the late afternoon light. When she glanced up at him, the sun caught her eyes and made the green flecks in her irises glow.

Hazel, he thought for the thousandth time. *Her eyes are hazel.*

Cal hoarded every little thing he knew about Elise with the rabid acquisitiveness of a dragon. If he could have turned what he knew into pearls, he would have kept the color of her eyes, the scent of her hair, the story behind the scar on her knee, and the way she sighed when he kissed her throat in the palm of his hand always.

He wanted all the pearls. He wanted the pearls to overflow from his hands, countless and infinitely precious, until they were all he could see and feel. He'd wondered if he would get bored by her by the end of their first week together, her novelty rubbed off like fog on glass, but it didn't happen. Not the first week. Not the second.

By their third week together, Cal was certain that he'd never tire of collecting those precious pearls, nor of kissing her, listening to her, *being* with her.

Always on the hunt for more, he asked, "You grew up here?"

"Yes. My parents moved here after the war ended, when they were still rebuilding a lot of downtown. Dad was a war correspondent, but after the charter was signed, he got a job at *The Light* and married my mom." Her eyes moved over the neat homes lining the quiet streets, a fond expression softening her face. "My sister Joanna came first, then my brother Liam." Her lips quirked in that sardonic smile he loved so much. "*I* was a surprise."

He could barely comprehend life in a family, let alone one as crowded as hers seemed to be. "Is it bad to be a surprise?" he asked, brow crinkling. He didn't like the idea of her being punished by the circumstances of her birth, no matter how hypocritical that was.

Elise gently bumped his arm with her shoulder. The end of her light scarf, a pale pink number with tassels on the end, lifted with the cool breeze. "Nah, but it is a running joke in the family. My brother is ten years older than me. They weren't expecting to have anymore kids, so it made for an interesting dynamic. My siblings were too old to be my playmates, so I mostly hung around my dad. He called me his kid reporter."

Cal looked down at her and felt a familiar, deep pang of hunger in his chest. Gods, he *wanted* this. Making the deal with Elise was both the best and worst thing he'd ever done. He couldn't imagine going back to a time when he didn't know the pleasure of touching her skin or feeling the radiance of her smile when he pleased her, when he gave her parts of himself he thought were worthless, when he ate the broccoli she hated or brought her small treasures from the ocean.

He wanted to walk under trees and hear about her family and feel her fingers intertwined with his every day for the rest of his life. Too bad he'd put a time limit on the greatest thing to ever happen to him. When the book finished, so too would they.

Cold dread trickled into his veins, as it always did when he thought about the words spilling across the screen of her monitor and what they represented.

She'd wanted to terminate their deal, and perhaps he should have let her. Maybe if they stopped this thing that day in her kitchen, he wouldn't feel like his whole world could be ripped out from under him at any second.

But, if the option presented itself, he knew he wouldn't change a thing. If he had to choose between heartbreak and a lifetime of frigid loneliness, he would choose heartbreak every time. At least now he knew what it felt like to be loved, to *live.*

"You don't have to worry about my parents," Elise assured him, misinterpreting his sudden silence for nerves. She gave his fingers a squeeze. "They're good people. Mom's a school teacher, so she's nice to pretty much everyone except my Uncle Chris — but that's because he's a bigot. Dad will probably grill you about where you're from, but only because he's obsessed with the city. If you let him ramble about history for a while, he'll think you're *great.*"

They took a left at a roundabout and passed a small park. Children and pets ran around the field and a small, colorful play structure, watched over by a group of eagle-eyed caregivers standing off to one side. One of the children had gauzy wings that caught the light and, upon closer inspection, he was fairly certain that wasn't a dog running with the small group, but a young coyote.

Elise caught him watching the scene with open curiosity and laughed. "Aren't they cute? This neighborhood used to be mostly arrants, but a lot of new families have moved in since they lifted that travel embargo." She nudged his arm and pointed across the street.

Cal turned his head and squinted at the brick house. The driveway was empty, and the small yard was impeccably maintained. A sloping path led from the sidewalk, through a fence with no gate, to a door with a symbol emblazoned on its face. It was a hand, palm forward, with an open eye in the center. He knew what it was, even if he'd never had the need to go to a place like it before. *A Healing House.*

"See? We even got a new healer recently. All the way from the Collective. I haven't met her yet, but my dad has been to see her a few times and says that she's managed to cure both his gout *and* his sweet tooth." She snorted. "Pretty sure he's using that to cover up the fact that he's sneaking sweets in his car again, but I'm not about to narc on him."

They passed the park and the Healing House before they turned right, onto another quiet street. Elise pointed again, this time at a small, white paneled home on a slight rise. Large, flowering hedges lined the driveway and where the lawn met the sidewalk. As they walked up the driveway, Cal caught sight of the sign above the door.

No solicitors. No crooks. No murderers — unless you're here for an interview.

He let out a low, raspy laugh. Of course Elise grew up here. He couldn't imagine her coming from anywhere else.

Following his stare, Elise explained, grinning, "An anniversary gift from my mom."

They stepped onto the porch. Cal felt a small burst of nerves — this was only the second time he was invited into a home before — but his curiosity quickly pushed them aside. "Anniversary? What's that?"

Elise waved her hand over the sensor on the door. A moment later, a chime sounded inside the house.

"Oh, it's what you call the day you got married or got together," she explained, looking up at him thoughtfully. "People like to celebrate how many years they've been together by giving each other gifts or doing something nice. Dad goes all out for their anniversary. Last year he took Mom on a river cruise through Eastern Europe. She came back raving about all the dragons she saw."

He heard a voice on the other side of the door, but he couldn't tear his eyes away from her face. Something pulled tight in his chest when he asked, "What will our anniversary be? The day you summoned me?"

Her eyes moved back and forth across his face as if she were searching for something. "I'm not sure," she answered, suddenly quiet. Watchful. "Having an anniversary usually means you're together for years, Cal. It's a... well, it's a sort of celebration of permanence."

That tight band across his heart pulled even tighter. *Right,* he thought bitterly, *and I set a fucking time limit on our relationship.*

Cal opened his mouth to inform her he had no intention of letting her go even after she finished the damn book, to tell her he wanted this kind of life with her, to say how desperately he wanted her, but he didn't get the chance. The front door swung open, forcing him to swallow the raw emotion bubbling up his throat.

Elise's parents were not what he expected. Her father was a

small, compact man with thick glasses and a dense, salt and pepper mustache. He wore a flannel shirt tucked into wrinkled khakis and had what appeared to be permanent frown lines etched into his forehead.

Her mother was taller than her father. Willowy, with the same athletic frame as her daughter, she had a long, kind face and a cap of short, silvery curls. He could feel the magic radiating off of her almost immediately. It was a stormy, chilly sort of power that he knew well.

Both, he noted, had a small, long-healed sigil burned between their brows.

"Oh, goodness gracious, baby," her mother exclaimed, laughing nervously. "You didn't tell me you were bringing a supermodel home for dinner! I would have put on something other than my old jeans."

Cal glanced down at Elise to find her cheeks flushing a familiar dark red. "Mom, Dad, this is Cal. Cal, these are my parents, Bob and Rachel."

He didn't know what to do, so Cal defaulted to his usual habit of keeping quiet. Squeezing Elise's hand, he gave them both a small nod.

After a moment of awkward silence, Bob put his hands on his hips and barked, "Quiet one! Gonna have to find that voice if you want to be Elise's boyfriend, kid. She needs someone with a spine!"

Elise and her mother wore identical expressions of mortification. "Dad, please do not—"

"I am not her boyfriend," Cal calmly explained. He didn't like talking to people, but in this he wanted there to be no confusion or room for doubt. Holding eye contact with her father, he announced, "I am her *mate.*"

Chapter Twelve

"You're going to tell me why you didn't mention that you'd found a mate in the most strikingly attractive man on the planet *soon,* right?"

Elise was impressed by her mother's restraint. She'd held her tongue all throughout the awkward, pre-dinner smalltalk phase and even through dinner itself. Only now that she stood alone in the kitchen, packing the leftover cake her father shouldn't have into a to-go container did her mother pounce.

"It's complicated, Mom." Knowing that wouldn't satisfy her — or anyone, really — Elise snapped the lid on the container and added, "We just met a few weeks ago. Things are new."

Her mother leaned her hip against the old kitchen island and crossed her arms, her expression skeptical. "Uh-huh. Is that why that elemental looks like he'll die if he doesn't touch you every five minutes? Seems like he's pretty certain about things."

"Well, yeah. I'm his first relationship."

Elise kept her eyes down, afraid that if her mother looked too closely, she would see how well and truly fucked her daughter's heart was. No, she didn't intend to just give Cal up, but he also hadn't said anything about the future beyond the book she was supposed to be writing. If he wanted to stick around, he would have said something. Cal was *always* direct, which was why she was having this conversation with her mother in the first place.

He said *'I'm her mate'*, but with him that could mean anything. She didn't know if elementals had permanent, monogamous relationships or if Cal even truly wanted one. She did her best to push the thought of him leaving her aside, but it was getting harder and harder to do so. Perhaps that was the real reason she hadn't yet made it clear that their deal meant nothing to her. Without it, she would be forced to face the truth: Cal might not actually want to stay.

Her mother's warm hand slid down her back. Dropping a kiss to the crown of Elise's head, she said, "I don't think that means as much as you probably think it does, sweetheart."

Tears threatened, but Elise stubbornly refused to let them fall. If she started crying out her heartache and worry now, her mother would never let her leave the house.

Instead of weeping like she was sixteen and just got stood up on homecoming night by Daniel fucking Kerber again, she leaned into her mother's embrace with a grateful hum. "We'll figure it out," she promised them both.

"I'm sure you will." Her mother straightened and brushed the hair out of Elise's eyes. "Well, if it makes any difference, I like him. A little grim, maybe, but I think that's good for you. It'll keep you out of too much trouble."

Elise let out a watery laugh. "I don't know what you're talking about. I never get into trouble."

"Uh-huh. And that's how you've ended up with a mysterious, brooding elemental for a boyfriend, right?"

She winced. "Fair enough."

Goddess help her if her mother ever found out what she'd done to get Cal's attention in the first place. They had agreed it was best for this first meeting to go without the explanation of who exactly Cal was, but the moment the truth came out, Elise was certain her mother would put the pieces together.

Smiling her wide, beautiful smile, her mother gave her back

another gentle rub before shooing her out of the kitchen. "You should go rescue him from your dad's lecturing by offering him a tour of the annex."

Elise frowned. "But what about the dishes?"

"It's Bob's night to do the dishes." Her mother shrugged. "Not my problem."

They shared an impish smile. "Did you plan on having us over on his dish night so you wouldn't have to do it?"

"I admit to nothing." Her mother waved a hand towards the door. "Shoo! Go get that pretty, pretty man!"

FROM THE DESK OF ELISE SASINI, A NOTE IN THE MARGIN OF THE MANUSCRIPT *THE SHROUDED CITY:*

I am so totally fucked.

By the time Elise found her father and his silent companion, her stomach was bunched up in a series of tight knots. They didn't loosen until Cal's eyes snapped to hers. He stood up abruptly from the old leather guest chair in her father's office, cutting off whatever Bob had been going on about. The crime rate in the 1930's, probably.

"Hey Dad," she greeted, pushing her hair behind her ear and avoiding Cal's hard, penetrating stare, "Mom says it's your dish night."

Her father let out a deep sigh that ruffled his mustache and slowly levered himself up from the chair behind his old, cluttered desk. After an awkward start, he'd warmed up to Cal. She suspected it had a lot to do with the fact that Cal wouldn't think to stop him from rambling even if he went on for hours and hours. He was a damn good listener.

"We'll finish this later, Cal," Bob assured him. "Next time, I can show you the maps I mentioned. We know where all six boats are sunk in the—"

"Dad."

"Fine, okay!" He threw up his hands and, squeezing past where she stood in the doorway, he dropped a kiss onto the side of her head.

She watched him walk down the hall and, once he disappeared around the corner, listened to the familiar sounds of him and her mother chattering at one another. An unfamiliar ache bloomed in her chest. Would she have something like what her parents had? Someone to always come home to? Someone who knew her better than she knew herself?

Elise had been so busy chasing her career for so long, she'd never given it much thought. She *did* want that, though. She wanted someone to sit up with her as she pieced a story together late in the night, to worry about her when she chased a lead. She wanted to squabble over who got to eat the last slice of cake and the best temperature setting on the thermostat. She wanted someone to tease her and keep her on her toes.

She wanted that person to be Cal.

A cool hand cupped her cheek. Elise looked up to find Cal staring down at her, his expression unreadable. Her brow wrinkled. She supposed Cal *was* broody, but her mother was right. Tonight, he didn't just look aloof. He looked downright grim. She'd been so in her head during dinner that she'd barely noticed his tension.

"Hey," she whispered, leaning into the hard, sleek lines of his body, "I bet you're feeling pretty overwhelmed with all this attention. Why don't we go some place quiet before we take the m-lev home?"

Cal was quiet for a moment, his eyes an impenetrable liquid black, before he answered, "Show me."

Elise took his hand and led him down the hall and through the back door, into the fenced in garden. Large hedges stood taller than the fence, giving the area a quiet, isolated feeling. Her mother's vegetable garden stretched along the pebbled path leading to the small building at the far end of the yard. Sprouts were just beginning to poke through the rich brown soil.

"What is this?"

"We call it *the annex,"* she explained, using the ancient thumb scanner to unlock the door. They had no reason to bother updating any of the tech in the little building, since it stood more as a monument to her childhood than a usable space. She had to actually flip a switch to turn on the lights when she stepped inside. A pink lamp on the table next to the bed turned on, as well as an electrician's nightmare of snarled and carelessly draped string lights.

Stepping inside, she let Cal in before she closed the door. His eyebrows rose.

"It's a lot of pink and purple, I know," she laughed. "This was my play house, since there wasn't much room for kiddy stuff in the house by the time I came along, and then when I was old enough, they converted it into my room." She took a sweeping look at the soft pink walls and the gaudy, shimmery curtains. The building itself was tiny — more of a shed than anything — but she wouldn't change a thing about it.

Growing up in a house where everyone was so much older and beyond her reach hadn't felt quite so isolating when she had her own special space to just be as silly and carefree as she wanted to. Besides, it was the place where *The St. Francis Chronicle* was born. She was pretty sure that if her parents tried to change it into a yoga studio or a deluxe garden shed, the historical society would sue their pants off.

At the very least, she would be terribly disappointed.

Elise started to tell him about the greatest accomplishment of her childhood, her beloved paper, but stopped as soon as she noticed the low mist beginning to circle the fuzzy purple carpet.

"Cal?"

He stood in the center of the small space. His back was to her, but she could tell something was wrong by the stiffness of his shoulders and the way his hair swayed back and forth like an angry wave.

His low voice was like a whip cracking through the silence when he said, "How come you didn't tell them I am your mate?"

She blinked. Had that been bothering him the whole night? She'd assumed his chilly reserve was caused by the unfamiliar company, not *that.* "Cal..." She struggled to come up with the right words. Ones that wouldn't give away how much she desperately wanted to keep him and ones that wouldn't push him away, either. Relationships were so new to him, she couldn't bear to influence him one way or the other. And, if she were being honest, she was scared to the bone that giving up the act would put an end to their relationship.

But she couldn't lie to him, either, so instead she said, "You and I are just starting out. I wasn't going to put that kind of pressure on you."

Cal spun around and pinned her with a dark look. "You are my mate. That was the agreement."

A spark of annoyance firmed up her spine. She wanted nothing more than to forget about that stupid, stupid deal, but he wouldn't *let her!* It hurt that he seemed to only care about their relationship in the context of the deal, and that hurt came out in her voice. "Well, what was I going to say, Cal? *This is my mate, but only until after I finish writing a book?* There was no way I was going to explain that to my parents!"

Cal was in front of her in the blink of an eye. Fog billowed around the room, obscuring every bit of pressed glitter and hot pink decor. The string lights twinkled through the gossamer mist, creating a dreamlike quality that was at odds with the tension between them.

He bore down on her with an expression of pure hurt when he hissed, "No anniversary. No telling them you're my mate. What's next? I told you I wanted *everything,* Elise. This is not everything. This is some... some *half* thing, and I don't want it."

Guilt twisted the knots in her stomach tighter. She'd been so careful with him, trying to show him that she cared and that it wasn't *really* about the book or the deal or any of that nonsense, but she'd also kept from mentioning the future for fear that he would tell her he had every intention of leaving her.

But that was selfish. The only real way to keep from hurting Cal was to cut him off at the beginning, before he got too deep into something he couldn't wrap his head around yet. He couldn't comprehend the mess they could make of one another, but she did. It was her responsibility to keep control of things. Instead of sticking to her guns and ending things before they began, she'd let him convince her to make an even bigger mess because she didn't actually want to stop.

Her throat was thick with withheld tears when she asked, "Do you want to end things, then?"

Cal went very still. "End things?"

She sucked in a shuddering breath. Damn, she'd done this to herself, but that didn't make it any easier to take. "This is confusing and obviously painful for you, which is what I worried about when we... started. I don't want you to be hurt, Cal." Her voice broke on his name, but she pushed ahead anyway. "If you want to end things now, then—"

Cal cut her off with a brutal, breath stealing kiss. His hands circled her waist and drew her close enough to plaster them together chest to thigh. One hand came up to curl into her hair, holding her still as he pressed one desperate kiss to her mouth after another.

"No, no, no," he panted against her lips. "I'm not ready to let you go. I can't do it. I *won't* do it."

Elise's will crumbled to so much dust, as it always did when she felt the ache in him. Gods, she couldn't leave this man. She didn't want to. She needed to just tell him she didn't care about the book or the deal and that she wanted him to *really* be her mate. Once that was out of the way, they could move forward — one way or the other.

Cal didn't give her the chance.

He slid his tongue along the seam of her mouth and then past it, stroking hers with a possessive caress. She didn't think anyone liked kissing as much as Cal did. Certainly, no one she'd ever kissed did it half as well as he did.

The hand on her waist slid under the hem of her shirt and up the bare expanse of her back, sending a new and exciting ripple of sensation down her spine. The shock of feeling his bare skin on hers made her gasp.

So far, she'd been very careful not to go past kissing with Cal. She knew he was eager for more — it was hard not to notice when the man eschewed clothing most days — but Elise was the one with the experience. She knew it was her responsibility to make sure he didn't go too far, too fast, and overwhelm himself. She'd always been careful to watch his cues, looking for signs that he was ready to move onto the next step, but he'd never shown any.

Not until now, anyway.

Desire wiped away her tension, the urgency she felt to just *tell* him. Unfulfilled, it had only gotten darker, sweeter as the weeks wore on. When Cal moved his hand to slide his fingers under the cup of her bra, Elise leaned into his touch. When he groaned, low and throaty, at the feeling of her tight nipple between the pads of his fingers, she dropped her hands to the waistband of his jeans.

When she popped the button and carefully pulled down the zipper, he hissed and pulled back from their kiss. Panting, he rasped, "What are you doing?"

Elise cupped his cheek with one hand and slid the other under the elastic band of his briefs, her eyes on his, watching for any sign of hesitancy or discomfort. When she brushed her fingertips over the silky skin of his shaft, he sucked in a ragged gasp that nearly unwound her. She clenched her thighs, assailed by a relentless, brutal desire.

"You said you wanted everything," she whispered, kissing the corner of his mouth with the utmost care. "Baby, I haven't even *started* giving you everything yet."

She curled her fingers around him and squeezed gently. His hips jerked. The hand in her bra spasmed, pinching her nipple sharply. A streak of pleasure raced down her spine to join the aching beat between her legs.

Gods, he felt like heaven in her hand. Heavy and silky, with all that perfect, pearlescent skin flushed *almost* pink. Elise had exactly zero doubts that he'd taste like heaven, too.

Cal stared down at her, lips parted and slick. His chest moved up and down with every deep inhale and exhale. "I want it," he breathed, voice hoarse with lust. "I want it all, witch."

Chapter Thirteen

FROM THE DESK OF ELISE SASINI, AN EXCERPT OF THE MANUSCRIPT *THE SHROUDED CITY:*

...on the subject of elementals as a whole, there is not much I can write. There is not much anyone can say for certain, as a matter of fact. Research in the subject is painfully lacking, but I cannot say I blame elementals for their circumspection. Perhaps, like the elves, they prefer to keep their secrets, their weaknesses and their wants, just that: secret.

Cal tells me that they are generally solitary, but he has only met a handful and cannot be entirely certain. He does not know if they mate for life or if they typically eschew permanent familial bonds. He doesn't know if they can have children, or if they all eat food, or if they sleep.

What he can tell me is his personal experience, and, I am ashamed to say, it is only his experience I am concerned with.

Fascinatingly, he confessed that, although he gained his physical form that disastrous morning in 1906, he'd actually achieved a level of sentience long before then. Wandering over the Earth as an amorphous cloud of magic, he remembers his first thought as, "Well, what are they all doing down there?"

I wonder, do the m-weather scientists know that the clusters of magic they study might actually be studying them back?

As an aside, I asked Cal whether this made him 139 years old, or many thousands. He thoughtfully replied, "Depends on whichever you like more."

Gods, I love him.

CAL KNEW WHAT SEX WAS. HE'D NEVER *DONE* IT, obviously, but one didn't hover in back alleys and linger around windows in a city like San Francisco for a hundred years *without* learning a thing or two about sex.

On the whole, he'd always considered it gross.

What were people thinking, plunging their tongues and fingers and genitals in places they didn't rightly belong? He understood the concept of copulation as well as its purpose, but as someone conceived by nothing other than magic and fate, Cal felt no compulsion to explore what Kaz playfully called *the carnal delights.*

Now, though, Cal wished he hadn't tuned out his friend when he tried to explain the joys of sex and intimacy all those years ago. Perhaps if he'd listened, he wouldn't be standing there, staring agog at his mate as she slowly lowered herself to her knees before him.

Doubtful, he thought wryly. In all likelihood, he would still look at her like she'd hung the moon. Even if he'd slept with every willing being in the city, this moment would still feel special. *Important.*

Elise slid her free hand under his shirt. Her palm pressed against the clenching muscles of his abdomen as she gave his cock a long, slow stroke. "Is this okay?" she asked, petting his stomach in time with her strokes. His heart swelled with the strangest mix of tenderness and borderline painful arousal he could imagine.

He wanted more.

"Yes." Cal felt her breath ghost over the sensitive head of his cock and groaned, low and long. He was so damn hard, he could

feel his heartbeat throbbing against the softness of her palm. "I've never done— *this.* I want to."

Gods, he wanted to do *everything* with her. Cal just never knew where to start. He loved kissing her more than he loved anything, but he knew there were more steps to the dance she had only begun to teach him. Was he supposed to do something to show he wanted to do *more* or was that something she needed to do? Was he missing some signal? Did he need to wait for her to tell him explicitly that they could go ahead with whatever it was that came next?

He had been on the verge of breaking down and seeking out Kaz for advice, but now that seemed unnecessary. Cal wasn't entirely certain what his witch had been waiting for, but that was a conversation for later. *After.*

It wasn't like he had any plans to let her go, anyway. Screw the terms of their deal. He'd find a way to keep her. They would have plenty of time to discuss this new facet of their relationship.

Even when he slid his fingers into her hair and felt the sweep of her tongue down his shaft in every single nerve ending, Cal felt the low hum of fury, of possessiveness in his blood. It wasn't easy keeping his shape together, and he had no control over the fog that billowed out to fill the tiny annex, obscuring the sight of them from anyone looking through the windows.

Do you want to end things, then?

Gods, he felt his heart stop when she said that. He wasn't ready for this to end. He wasn't ready to go back to how he was before. He wasn't ready to not see her every day, to not hear her voice, to not kiss her whenever the mood struck him. He wouldn't ever be ready.

Cal wasn't sure if elementals had mates. Not every race did. Humans, certainly, didn't seem to have some ingrained compulsion to stick with one partner for all time. Elementals were solitary. They didn't do packs or families. They came into the world alone and they died alone.

But he wanted more than that. She taught him that he *deserved* more than that.

He wanted Elise Sasini, the woman on her knees before him, her lips running down the length of his cock in a reverent caress, and he intended to have her. *Forever.* He was prepared to fight her tooth and nail to make it happen.

He watched her with unvarnished hunger. Elise was beautiful and smart and kind and she was *his.* Her lips were flushed a bright cherry red. They looked even more lush, more human, when they were pressed against his pearly white skin.

Cal shifted his stance, moving his booted feet so she could have more room. Wanting to see her face, he gathered her hair in one fist and held it back. It was a soft, heavy weight in his hand, and he relished the feeling of it.

"Tell me if you want to stop or if you're uncomfortable," she murmured, sliding her hand slowly back up his length to press the pad of her thumb against the underside of the flushed head. Elise kept her eyes on his as her tongue darted out to lick up a gleaming drop of pre-come.

Cal's fist tightened around her curls. *Gods save me.*

"Deal?"

He got his answer out through gritted teeth. "Deal."

Her smile was beautiful. Cal never got tired of seeing it. He'd been the subject of many grateful, nervous, or vacant smiles throughout his lifetime, but he'd never seen a grin like Elise's. It was huge and radiant; a smile that took up her whole face and crinkled her eyes until they were just little slits of glittering hazel. Whenever she blessed him with one, Cal felt like the weight of a century fell off of his shoulders. Her joy made him feel *new.*

And when she beamed up at him from her position on the floor, her cheeks flushed and her magic calling out a siren song to his, he discovered a new appreciation for it. There was an entirely new world of satisfaction to discover in the joy she took in the task at hand.

Cal's breath quickened as she began to press one achingly

tender kiss after another along his shaft, her eyes locked on his. He didn't know what to do with his other hand, so he settled for cupping her cheek.

Another wave of pleasure crashed over him when he realized he could *feel* her jaw and tongue work as she showered him with touches. It was made even more clear — and arousing — when she finally took him into the slick heat of her mouth.

"Elise!" Cal's spine stiffened as she slowly closed her lips over him. The slick, velvety pad of her tongue stroked the underside of his cock as she drew him in.

Stars exploded behind his eyes. Cal gasped, head dropping back, and held on for dear life as Elise began to move forward and back. Her lips and tongue created a maddening suction and heat, while her hand moved in time, taking over whatever she couldn't reach with her mouth.

There was something dangerously erotic about feeling her cheek hollow out under his palm. He didn't need to *see* her to know exactly what she looked like. He could feel it and hear it.

Cal rocked his hips in time with her. He knew enough to keep himself from letting go completely, but he was shocked to discover his restraint wearing away under the onslaught of pleasure. He had no idea it could *do* that. Sure, he assumed sex felt good — why else would so many people go to such great lengths to do it? — but *this...*

It was like she was taking him apart piece by piece with nothing more than the heat of her mouth and her wicked fingers. He thought he knew carnal pleasure when they kissed for the first time, but it was *nothing* compared to this. Gods, would he ever be able to look at her mouth the same? Or would he forever see his pearlescent skin sliding between her flushed lips, taboo and beautiful and everything he never knew he needed?

Pressure began to build at the base of his spine, pulling every single one of his muscles taut. Cal made a choked sound in the back of his throat and gave her hair a gentle pull, telling her he needed her to stop. If she kept going, he was certain he'd come apart at the seams. It was too much.

Elise withdrew her head, but kept her fingers wrapped firmly around his cock when she asked, husky and breathless, "Are you okay, baby?"

Gods, her voice was rough. He'd heard it like that before, after he'd kissed her breathless. It'd done things to him then, but *now,* with his cock in her hand, it did a whole lot more.

Cal tilted his head down to look at her and groaned again. She was so fucking beautiful it nearly killed him. Did she honestly think he could live the rest of his life without her now? Without *this?* He'd wither away into senseless, formless mist without her. He'd *want* to.

"I'm— it's too much," he rasped. "It feels..." He didn't even have the words to finish the sentence. It felt fucking incredible, but even that was inadequate.

A slow, sultry smile curled Elise's wet lips. "Are you close?"

Cal blinked. "Close?"

She tightened her grip and gave his cock a slow, torturous pull. Cal made a noise of pained surprise as he watched another milky drop of pre-come slide down the tip. Before it could run over her fingers, Elise's tongue snaked out to swipe it away with careful, deliberate slowness. He watched it melt on her pretty pink tongue. Her gaze never left his face.

Tempest take me to the depths. This woman is going to kill me.

"Orgasm, baby," she explained, eyes crinkling with her smile. "Are you close to orgasming?"

Cal felt like he couldn't get enough air in his lungs. He felt like every nerve had been shot with electricity. He felt like every drop of blood in his body now belonged in his cock. He felt like he would die if she stopped and like he would *definitely* die if she continued.

"I... don't know," he managed to get out. "I've never— This isn't something I've—"

It was Elise's turn to look surprised. Sitting back a little, she used her free hand to rub soothing circles over his hip bone. "Oh, Cal. You've never had an orgasm before? Not even on your own?"

He shook his head.

"Oh, *baby.*" Elise leaned forward to press a tender kiss to his stomach. Her tone was achingly gentle when she said, "That's okay. This is all normal. Do you *want* to keep going?"

Cal swallowed hard. He was overwhelmed, but he knew he wanted this. He wanted her. "Yes."

She kissed him again. Pride glowed in her flushed face and made his heart ache. "Do you trust me?"

"Yes." He trusted Elise in ways he'd never trusted anyone. Never, in all of their interactions, had she shown anything other than care and affection for him. Even when he was angry and confused and lonely, she *cared* for him. Always patient, always funny, always practical. She was the steady ground on which he stood, the only thing that made sense to him in the world. She was his *home.*

Elise gave his cock another slow, reverent stroke. He rocked his hips and let out a small whine. The pressure had only abated temporarily. Every time she moved or even *breathed* near his sensitive skin, Cal felt like he was going to explode.

"Good," she breathed, peppering his stomach with kisses. She'd rucked up his plain black shirt and seemed to find it pleasurable to trace the contours of his abdomen with her lips and tongue. He couldn't complain. Having her mouth on him *anywhere* was bliss.

Resting her chin on his stomach for a moment, she looked up at him with an open, tender expression that stole what little breath he still had. "You're going to be okay, baby. It's going to feel like a lot, like you're going to come apart, but you can trust me. It will be good. If not, we never have to do this again, okay? I'm right here with you."

His fist tightened in her hair. "Do you promise?"

Moisture glittered in those pretty hazel eyes. Her smile softened. "Yes, Cal. I promise."

Only when he nodded did she finally dip her head back down. He let out something close to a shout when her lips closed over him again. Her left hand drew comforting patterns on his stomach and side as she sucked, gently at first, then harder and faster, her right hand working in tandem with her mouth with a pulling, twisting motion.

His blood rushed with a pulsing beat. It was a roar in his ears, overpowering his own involuntary moans and the slick, erotic sound of her mouth on him. That pressure returned with a vengeance. It pulled and pulled and pulled, curling his toes in his boots and forcing a raw, terrifying noise from his throat.

And then the tension snapped.

Cal cried out, hips bucking hard, and grasped the sides of her head to still her movements as bursts of pure pleasure rocked him to the core.

When there was nothing left of him, he felt his muscles unlock, his shoulders sagging and his eyelids falling shut as he finally, *finally* got some air back in his lungs.

The feeling of soft, warm fingers gently tucking him back into his briefs and then rubbing soothing circles over his hips and thighs brought him back to the present.

Cal blinked hard, dispelling the little white lights that danced across his vision, to see Elise grinning up at him. As he watched, dumbstruck, her tongue snaked out to catch a drop of come from escaping the corner of her mouth. She winked up at him.

"Gods, I love blowjobs," she murmured, "but that has got to be the single best sexual experience of my fucking life." Her eyes glittered. "And next time it will be even *better.*"

He dropped to his knees. There was nothing else he could do. His legs certainly wouldn't support him anymore. He wasn't even sure they were fully corporeal. Not that he cared. If she asked it of him, he would have even *crawled.*

Cupping her cheeks, Cal leaned forward to breathe against her swollen mouth, "You're going to kill me, witch."

She bumped her nose against his, playful and sweet and too

good for him. Too bad he was past worrying about that. He was a murderer and a monster and he'd rot in the mud of Grim's riverbank, but he was fucking *hers.*

Elise pressed a soft kiss to his lips. He felt her smile against them when she said, "Well, death's not really what I'm after—"

A powerful, percussive wave knocked them both to the ground. Cal threw himself over Elise as trinkets and baubles began to rain down from the shelves around the room. His ears rang with a single, high note as he curled his arms around her, blocking any shards of glass from reaching her fragile skin.

A series of smaller explosions rent the air, one after another; several distant booms that shook the annex's thin walls. In total, it only lasted a minute or two, but with the fear for Elise coursing through his veins like ice water, it might as well have been a lifetime.

Only when he was sure that it was over did Cal cautiously lift his head to examine the room. Elise pushed at him, wiggling to be let up, but he needed to know that the roof wasn't about to fall on her before he allowed her out from under him.

When a cursory scan found only minimal damage to things not bolted to the walls, he reluctantly let her crawl out from under him. "Watch the glass. You'll cut your hands," he warned.

"My hands! Screw my hands!" Elise shook her head and surged to her feet. Two strides took her to the door. "Was that an *explosion* or some insanely massive bolt gun shots? Gods, I have to go check on my parents!"

Cal followed her mad dash back through the garden and into the house. The afterglow of their time in the annex was wiped away by the sight of a living room full of glass — all from the broken windows, which had apparently blown *inward* — and Rachel attempting to help Bob up from where he knelt on the floor by the couch.

Elise rushed over to help. Putting a shoulder under her father's arm, she asked, "Are you guys okay? What happened?"

Frowning, Cal gently extracted her from under her father and took her place. Using his greater strength, he managed to get Bob onto the couch with minimal jostling.

Rachel stood by the armrest and shook her head. She looked shaken, but unharmed. Bob didn't look much worse, save for a small cut to the side of his head and a muttered complaint about his bum knee. "I don't know!" Elise's mother answered. "We were just turning on an entertainment feed when the windows shattered."

Elise grabbed a fistful of the back of Cal's shirt and leaned around him to peer out the window. The flush in her cheeks died away. "Oh, fuck me," she breathed, "there's a fire! Gods, I *told* the association that those old gas lines needed to be removed."

Cal straightened, his mouth settling into a grim line. They shared a look.

Elise sucked in a deep breath and nodded once, firmly, toward the door. She gave him a gentle shove. "Go."

Chapter Fourteen

FROM THE DESK OF ELISE SASINI, A TRANSCRIPT OF AN AUDIO RECORDING DATED FEBRUARY 8th 2045:

ELISE: Can— can we circle back to... back around to what you said before. About your vigil.

CALAMITY: What about it?

ELISE: I'm wondering why you do it. What it really entails. Also, I guess, how it plays into what you told me about people trying to use you over the years. Thaddeus in particular.

[PAUSE] [FABRIC SOUNDS] [CHAIR LEGS SCRAPING]

ELISE: Oh! Cal, I don't think—

CALAMITY: I will answer your questions, but only if I get to hold you while I do it. This is part of the deal.

ELISE: ...Right. Comfy?

CALAMITY: Yes. Here are the answers to your questions: I do it because it's my penance. It usually means I keep watch over the city and its surrounding area for danger. I save every life I can — from drowning, assault, house fires, car accidents. It's all the same. [PAUSE] Lay your head on my shoulder. Yes. I like it when you do that.

[FABRIC SOUNDS]

ELISE: [SIGH] Go on.

CALAMITY: The Mad Sovereign was no different from anyone else, except that he actually had the power to force my hand. For a while, anyway. He wanted me to be a part of his shadow Patrol. In his eyes I would be the perfect assassin and spy. Most people who seek me out think the same. Usually they try to offer money, sex, influence. When that doesn't work, they resort to threats, then violence. He was the only one who got close to beating me into it. I've never felt pain like what that man gave me before or since.

ELISE: Oh, Cal...

CALAMITY: [MUFFLED] Shh, witch. All's well. He lost his head. My only regret is that I wasn't the one to take it from him.

~

THERE WAS NO SAVING THE HEALING HOUSE. CAL knew it the moment he shed his clothes and his physical form to spread himself out to catch the air. He didn't need to go far to find the blaze.

The Healing House was only about a block down from Elise's childhood home and it was burning down to its foundations. As he watched, hovering over the blaze, the damaged roof caved in with a crash and a roar of hungry flame. If there were people inside, they were already dead.

Feeling the tight knot of guilt that never let him go, Cal searched the area around the building for survivors before he committed himself to helping extinguish the blaze.

A lone figure lay prone on the brick path leading to the door. Her pastel colored coat stood out starkly against the smoke and debris. Relief surged through him. Not all was lost. He could save one person, at least. It didn't scrub any marks from his soul, but it didn't add another one, either.

Cal made to swoop down, intending to pull the woman out of harm's way, but reared back in surprise when black, faceless shadows melted from the gaps between the houses. One of the black-clad figures — broad shouldered, with a smoky glamour disguising any distinguishing features — knelt by her side and briskly checked her for injuries. More figures knelt down beside her and others stood watch, their backs ramrod straight and their obscured faces turned toward the road.

Sovereign's Guard.

He could hardly believe what he was seeing. A full squadron — six elves, trained to work in seamless pairs — of the most highly trained, dangerous military force in the UTA were crowded around the fallen woman. No one but the sovereign commanded the Guard. That meant that, whoever the woman was, Theodore Solbourne ordered her surveillance personally.

Cal watched as they relayed information to one another with quick, efficient hand signs, then the figure who had checked for injuries lifted a hand to his ear.

Over the roar of flames and the distant wail of sirens, Cal heard, "Explosion at the Healing House. No combatants. Healer down but alive. Do we extract?"

People were beginning to exit their homes. Terrified neighbors peeked out of doorways and called out to one another from across the street. Somewhere, the wails of distressed pets were joined by a baby.

In a moment, people would begin to venture out in earnest. Already, Cal could hear the fire squad closing in. Would the Guard stay? They were supposed to work in the shadows, never seen except for at the sovereign's elbow. A full squadron being caught surveilling a Healing House had to be high on their list of things to avoid.

The glamoured voice of the guard was crisp and emotionless when he replied to whoever he spoke to. "Understood. Awaiting further instructions."

With a sharp gesture, the elf sent the rest of the squadron back into the shadows. Long, loping strides allowed them to disappear in the few seconds it took for the only guard left to gently lift the unconscious woman and deposit her at the farthest end of the path, nearly on the sidewalk. It was far enough away to keep her out of immediate danger from the burning building, but close enough to look as though she landed there on her own.

Carefully, like she was made of something more fragile and precious than spun glass, the guard laid her head on a patch of grass. With a flick of his matte black claw-caps, he made sure her skirt and coat were arranged around her legs in a way that concealed the most possible skin before he too stood and raced back to the cover of shadows.

In all, the entire bizarre scene took less than a minute.

If Cal had his physical form, he would have shaken his head. He never could make sense of the elves or what they wanted. Why not take the woman out of danger entirely? Why arrange her like they did? Why have a full squadron of elite soldiers watching her in the first place?

It didn't sit right with him, but he didn't have the time to consider what it all might mean. As a human neighbor raced over to help the fallen woman, Cal turned his attention to the burning house. He'd seen enough over the years to know that flames had a mind of their own, particularly in a magic saturated city like San Francisco. They could jump and weave and come back to life without any warning. If the blaze wasn't handled soon, it could consume the entire neighborhood, if not the whole city.

Thinking of Elise's childhood home and her little annex, Cal pulled his magic inward before releasing it in one big burst. Immediately, fog began to coalesce in the air, pulled from every bit of moisture he could get his incorporeal hands on. He couldn't put out the flames entirely, but he could help dampen them until the fire squad arrived.

As people poured out into the street and the battered woman was escorted away by two neighbors, Cal pressed himself as close to the flames as he dared. He was impervious to most damage in his dematerialized form, but heat could burn him as surely as it could if he were flesh and bone. It was the one weakness Thaddeus had been able to exploit, and it had taken him decades to get past the terror flames inspired in him. Only his need to save lives had pushed him past the pain of his memories. Of course, the process was helped along by a heaping helping of spite for the dead madman, too.

A thick layer of fog rolled over the neighborhood to blanket what was left of the Healing House. By the time the fire squad arrived, the flames were hissing and popping under the onslaught of moisture; smothered to death beneath a blanket of unnatural fog.

Cal worked in tandem with the foam-throwing squad, though they didn't know it. It took fifteen minutes for them to get the blaze under control. By then, Cal felt it was safe to let the professionals handle what was left of the smoldering building.

Curious, he lingered over the street and watched as first the alpha of the local coyote shifter pack arrived with his second, and then, in perhaps the most bizarre turn of events he could imagine, the sovereign himself stepped out of a sleek black car.

He'd never met Theodore Solbourne and didn't care about the man one way or another, but even Cal felt a ripple of disquiet at the sight of his furious expression and flexing claws. Kaz, of course, was close behind him.

The orc didn't follow his brother over to the small knot of people sitting on the curb in front of the ruined house, but stayed a discreet distance away, half hidden in the shadow cast by a tree. One glance upward told Cal he knew he wasn't alone.

"Long time no see, Cal."

Not wanting to draw attention to himself, Cal half-materialized in the deepest shadows under the stooping tree. "What's going on?"

Kaz shifted his stance. He was ever-so-slightly bowlegged —

something that only made the massive orc look bigger than he was. Leather-clad arms crossed over his wide chest, he dryly answered, "Family shit."

Cal glanced across the street, where it looked like a stand-off was happening between the alpha and the sovereign. Why? Because of the little red-headed woman? He couldn't imagine what the Solbourne family had to do with the healer, or even the coyote shifter, for that matter. "What's so special about that woman?"

"She's family." It was a short, implacable answer. Nothing in Kaz's tone or expression hinted that he was open to more discussion on the topic. Not that Cal really cared or needed to know. A life had been saved and a neighborhood left relatively unscathed. His job was finished.

Shrugging, he eyed his only friend curiously. "I've been meaning to track you down."

Kaz shot him a quick, amused look. "You know where you can find me, fog man."

True, but Cal didn't care to waste any of his time with Elise checking Kaz's usual haunts. He shrugged. "I've been busy."

"With what?" It was more of a grunt than a question, but Cal didn't take offense. Kaz's direct, dry nature was one of the main reasons they were able to get along. When the newest regime took power, they were right to send their half-orc sibling to make contact with Cal. They were both emotionally stunted and brusque, making miscommunication almost non-existent.

"I met a woman."

The orc jolted. Tearing his eyes away from his brother, his head swiveled to pin Cal with a look of outright disbelief. "A woman? *Really?*"

"Yes," he answered, a bit defensive. "I have a mate now." He lifted his chin. "She is incredible. *No one* has a mate as good as mine."

Kaz's eyes widened. His brows, two inky black slashes, rose high on his forehead. "A mate."

Cal scowled. Was it so hard to believe that he'd found a mate? Given his history, perhaps the skepticism could be forgiven, but he still didn't like the shock on his friend's face. "That's what I said."

"When did this happen?"

"Almost three weeks ago." Cal shifted, the mist that was his lower body swirling with impatience. Truly, he didn't want to be standing there talking to Kaz. He wanted to be back with Elise, who would kiss him and fuss and needle him about every little fact he could recall about the events he witnessed.

Gods, he loved it when she spent hours and hours getting information out of him. He soaked up her attention like a damn sponge.

Still, he needed to talk to Kaz. He needed to know how to make their mating permanent, and the orc was the only person he trusted to give him good information on the subject.

"Damn. You've been mated three weeks and you wait until *now* to tell me?" He made a small sucking sound with his teeth, muttering, "Gotta get you a damn mating gift too, I guess."

"Yes, and I need to get back to her," Cal announced, waving a dismissive hand at whatever was going on across the street. "I only came to help with the fire. But I've been meaning to talk to you. I need information on mating."

Impossibly, Kaz's eyebrows crawled higher. "If you already have a mate, why—"

Impatient, Cal interrupted him to say, "Because she thinks it is only temporary, but it isn't. I need to know how to keep a mate and make sure she never leaves me."

"Only... temporary?" Kaz's eyes darted between the tense scene by the smoldering Healing House and Cal. Confusion was written in every line of his pretty orcish face. "That's not how mating works. Just what in Glory's name have you gotten yourself into, Cal?"

"I'm not sure. This is *why* I need your advice," he ground out.

Kaz shook his head. Long black hair, thick and wavy, swept back and forth over the back of his beaten leather jacket. "I'm not mated, Cal. I wouldn't know the first thing about it."

"But you know people who *are* mated," Cal pressed. "You know how it's supposed to work."

"I... Well, sure, I guess, but—"

Cal made a frustrated sound in the back of his throat. "Please, Kaz. I need help. You are my only friend. I trust you."

"Ah, fuck," the orc muttered, kicking a pebble at the tire of his parked car.

When he took too long to answer, Cal added, "She is all I've ever wanted. I can't lose her, Kaz. I won't survive it."

"Shit. Picked a real fucking time to fall in love, fog man." Kaz scrubbed his scarred knuckles over his jaw, his eyes on his brother's back. Theodore was leaning down to talk to the small woman, one gloved hand wrapped around the back of her neck in a possessive hold even Cal recognized.

Arching his brows, Cal glanced around to find more elvish shadows moving around the street. Residents were being ushered back into their homes, and a clean up crew had already begun to wipe all evidence of the incident from the street. By morning, he guessed that even the damage done to the surrounding homes would be fixed. No evidence left behind.

His eyes swung back to the sovereign and the woman he held. She didn't seem pleased to see him, but she wasn't trying to free herself from his hold, either. Petite and breakable looking, she still managed to stare up at the sovereign boldly, her fists clenched at her sides. Whatever it was the Solbournes were up to, Cal had a feeling that the healer wouldn't bend to their machinations easily.

"Fine." Kaz sighed, drawing Cal's attention back to important things. "But I'll need your help with something in exchange. Deal?"

For Elise, Cal would do anything. No questions asked. "Deal."

"Meet me at the bar. Midnight."

Cal nodded. Their business done, he let the rest of his form dematerialize once more.

Finally, he thought, catching the air currents that led back to Elise, *I'm going to get some answers.*

Chapter Fifteen

Elise stayed with her parents well into the night, citing the need to help them clean up and make sure they were all right. Cal didn't mind, though he would have preferred they were both back in her apartment. He'd adapted to having a home quickly. Rather than feeling confined like he thought he would, he'd only grown more possessive of the space and of the woman who resided there.

He couldn't say the same thing about her childhood home, though. Even after Bob and Rachel retired to their room, he felt uncomfortably restricted in the unfamiliar space. Cal was sure that part of it was due to the fact that things were oddly tense between Elise and himself.

There was too much to say, too much emotion roiling between them, and her family's home was not the place to safely work through the minefield between them. By silent agreement, they didn't bring up their previous conversation, nor the way Elise had completely shattered his world in the annex.

When he stood by the open back door, half-dematerialized and ready to escape the confines of his flesh and his frustrations for a while, they shared a look heavy with understanding.

"I'll see you at home," she whispered, stretching onto her tiptoes to brush a kiss across his lips.

Cal felt that peculiar pressure building again. It was an ache in his chest, like an acute longing for her had metastasized into real pain. He kissed her more firmly, always hungry for her, and reassured himself that, come tomorrow morning, he would have the tools necessary to renegotiate their deal. He would make her his. There was no other option.

The terms had changed. He didn't want a temporary mate. He wanted *forever,* and he'd go to any lengths necessary to get it.

FROM THE DESK OF ELISE SASINI, AN EXCERPT FROM THE MANUSCRIPT *THE SHROUDED CITY:*

Cal won't tell me about what exactly happened during his year in Solbourne custody. I don't blame him. My father was a war correspondent for nearly sixty years. After the war ended, he worked full time for The Light. *Being a journalist in the 1980's through the 2000's was a dangerous venture. Thaddeus II's crackdown on the press reached its peak then, and my father was one of many journalists to find themselves in the bowels of a Solbourne dungeon.*

My father was held for three months after writing an article about a series of disappearances around the city. He was bold — or foolish — enough to outright speculate that they were politically motivated, and he paid the price for it. My father won't talk about his time with the shadow Patrol, either, but it haunts him.

Like with Cal, I can see the truth that can't be spoken. My father's knee has never been the same, though he blames his pain on gout, and he hasn't taken his shirt off in front of anyone but my mother in forty-five years. Cal won't go near an open flame if he can help it, and I've started taking longer routes on the m-lev to avoid having to take him underground. He's never said a word, but when we glide through the tunnels, I can feel his fear sticking to me like a second skin.

I'm not sure if it's the abhorrence of pity or a desire to forget about their trauma that makes them reluctant to share the details of what happened to them. Maybe it's a protective urge to save their loved ones from knowledge that can only hurt them. I don't know.

Cal is open about other things, though. When I asked him how he feels about the current regime, he simply shrugged. He doesn't seem to hold any ill-will toward Theodore Solbourne or any of the Solbourne family. He is more forgiving than I am.

Cal's eyes, swaths of inky black, are placid when he explains, "They are not their father. I don't hold his sins against them anymore than you hold the sins of my birth against me, even if I think you should."

He is a tangle of contradictions, my mate. He is an eminently practical being, and as such, he is aware that his guilt is illogical, unfounded. When he says things like that, I am reminded again of his complexity — as well as my desire to throttle a select few people.

Guilt thrives in him, eating away at a soul that is good to its deepest foundations. If I could carve the guilt out of him with my hands, I would. I can't, though. Perhaps someday he will let me replace his oldest companion with something softer, kinder, but it is not today, nor tomorrow.

For now, all I can say is, "Tell me more about the people you've saved, Cal."

Chapter Sixteen

Kaz's favorite bar was a shithole called *The Broken Tooth.* Deep in the seediest part of the Tenderloin neighborhood, it was as unassuming as the shattered glass in the gutters. At four AM, a cleaning bot would sweep away the sins of the night from the street, but the bar would remain, and its patrons would simply replace what was swept up. Sometimes it was glass, usually it was cigarette butts, and occasionally it was blood. Even in the capital of the squeaky clean Protectorate, filth and violence would always have a foothold.

Cal understood why Kaz picked this particular dive bar as his favorite haunt. In the middle of a web of underground Markets — where black market goods, drugs, and desperate people passed from hand to hand — it was the perfect place for the head of the Solbourne's intelligence force to keep his eye on the pulse of the EVP.

Not many people knew that Kaz was perhaps the single most dangerous man in the territory, nor that he controlled a vast underground network of informants and spies. Even fewer knew that he was not just an orcish mercenary hired to keep the sovereign safe.

He was Theodore Solbourne's half brother, and despite his

outward appearance, he was every bit as elvish and single-mindedly ruthless as the rest of his family.

When Cal stepped into *The Broken Tooth's* hazy interior, he found Kaz sitting at the far end of the sticky bar, a green bottle of beer clasped loosely around the neck with two clawed fingers. Cal peered closely at his friend's hands, more curious about them than he'd ever been before.

Now that his focus had shifted to being mated, he was terribly curious about the subject on the whole. He only knew the bare minimum of orcish mating habits and nothing at all about elves, since they kept everything secret. That never bothered him before, but now he felt compelled to know more. Perhaps there was some secret to their success he could uncover if he dug far enough.

Sliding onto the stool next to his friend, Cal asked, "When you find your mate, your hands will turn black, yes? Like your claws?"

Kaz grunted and lifted his beer to his lips for a harsh swig. His claws, naturally glossy black, looked extra sinister against the glass of the bottle.

A staticky blues song played over the sound of low chatter. A hunched figure was smoking in a far corner, gaunt face turned toward an old feed screen showing the latest arena fight. With just a glance to his right, Cal could immediately tell that the three vampires sitting in a booth by the grimy window were having a *very* serious discussion. A look to his left took in the were woman behind the bar, her mismatched eyes keen and her face lined with age, as well as the patron she spoke to, a fellow were with shaggy brown hair and a pale, sweaty face.

Turning his attention back to Kaz, Cal thought, *The Solbournes don't even need me anymore.*

Truly, what use did they have for him when Kaz could blend in so well with the shadows and the people who dwelled there? No one in the bar would ever think he was half a step away from the Protectorate's throne.

The Solbourne family's enemies wouldn't think to be wary of

one single, intimidating orc in elvish territory. By the time they realized their mistake, it would be too late.

Lowering the bottle back onto the scratched bar top, Kaz curtly answered, "Yeah. Hands and feet. Why?"

Cal looked down at his own hands and scowled. "I want something like that. Then she would know every time she looks at me that I'm hers."

Kaz let out a low, weary rumble. "It's not all it's cracked up to be, you know."

"What do you mean?"

"The fated shit." Kaz's voice was its usual sonorous purr, but there was an edge of bitterness in it that Cal had never heard before. "The biological imperative bullshit. A lot of people revere it, but it's not like we're given a choice." He lifted his left hand and made a sharp, dismissive gesture with his fingers. "See this hand? It could take the kohl for anyone. I wouldn't get to choose, or decide I'm ready. One day, I'll walk into the wrong room or breathe in a scent from across a park and it'll just happen. Choice? Gone."

Cal drummed his fingertips on the bar top. His hair swirled over his shoulders as he worked through his confusion. "But doesn't that make things easier? If you know that person is your mate, there is no talking or deciding or negotiating. No *deals.*"

Kaz arched a dark, winged brow. "Deals?" He shook his head. "You think it's a simpler way, but it's not. Neither fate nor biology give a shit about anyone. You know what the kohl brought my mother? Fucking Mad Thad, a bastard, and an early death." Kaz paused to take another sip of his beer. Muttering into the rim, he added, "If I stay unmated for the rest of my life, it'll be a gods-damned blessing."

It was hard to argue with that, even though Cal heartily wanted to. Now that he new the comforts of a mate — the feeling of knowing he never had to be alone again, the bone-deep contentment of her nearness, the roar of lust when he was blessed with her touch — he thought that he might have a better grasp on the benefits than his friend did.

Of course he also understood the risks. He wasn't sure what it would be like to live your life knowing you could, at any second, have your health and happiness tied to a stranger. Cal counted himself extremely lucky that the only woman he'd ever desired was a good, compassionate, intelligent witch. It was entirely possible that Kaz would not be so lucky.

Of course he won't be as lucky as I am, he thought, sitting up a little straighter on his stool. *The best mate is already taken.*

"Well, whether you want a mate or not, *I* do," he said, firmly steering the discussion back where he needed it to be. "I need to know how to make Elise mine forever."

Kaz barked out a husky laugh. "You and every other lovesick motherfucker." He tipped his beer in Cal's direction and grinned. Large upper and lower fangs gleamed against the jewel tone of his skin even in the dim, smoky bar. "Tell me the story and I'll see if I can help."

When the bartender walked over to ask if he'd like something, Cal turned her down. He didn't eat or drink much at all. A meal every other month usually did the trick, and he preferred the taste of saltwater to any of the bottled bile Kaz loved to drink. Besides, if he did want to consume something, he vastly preferred to be with Elise when he did it.

When his friend had a fresh beer and the bartender walked back to the other end of the bar, Cal asked, "First, what do you want from me?"

It was a familiar game between them, this dance of negotiation and exchange of favors. It was how they came to be friends in the first place, though neither could pinpoint exactly when it happened with any sort of certainty.

Kaz ran his claws through his loose hair. He looked tired. "Lot going on back home," he explained. "I need you to keep an eye out for anyone talking about what happened at the Healing House tonight. Any word about a bomb, or someone looking to hire someone for a job. Anything, and I mean *anything,* about it or Margot Goode."

"Margot Goode?" Cal frowned. He knew who the Goodes were, but he'd never heard the first name before. "Who is that?"

His friend snorted, but Cal couldn't figure out what was funny about his question. "She was the healer in residence. The redhead who almost died tonight." He leaned in close and dropped his voice until Cal could barely hear it over the music. "She's family."

"You said that before." The longer he stared at Kaz's grim expression, the more a suspicion niggled at him. "She's not an elf, so she's..."

The orc inclined his head, his eyes hard. He looked pissed, and Cal finally began to understand why. "Teddy's."

Cal leaned back and blinked hard, absorbing the information. At the other end of the bar, the shaggy-haired were stood up and hustled out, his hands shoved into his pockets and his head down. The bartender darted out after him, a towel thrown over her shoulder, as she called, "Roger, wait! You can't just—"

They disappeared out the swinging door. Cal watched them go before he turned his attention back to his friend. "Someone tried to kill her?"

"Looks like."

Well, that cleared up the mystery of why the Sovereign's Guard were watching her house. If that little woman was Theodore Solbourne's mate, he pitied whoever tried to hurt her. Elves weren't exactly known for their mercy, nor their tolerance for threats. He would know.

"I'll help you however I can," he promised. He would have agreed to almost anything if it helped him keep Elise, but now that he was fighting for his own mate, he discovered a newfound kinship with the sovereign. If it were *his* mate in danger, he'd do far worse than ask for help from a friend.

Kaz reached back to clap him on the shoulder. The blow would have knocked a human man off of his stool. Cal wasn't human, but it still came close. "Thank you, fog man. We won't forget it." The orc gave his shoulder another wallop. "Now tell me about your mate."

"Her name is Elise Sasini," he proudly explained. "She's a *writer.*"

"Sasini?" It was Kaz's turn to lean back on his stool, his eyebrows arching high. "Daughter of Robert Sasini, the crime writer? International bestselling author of *A Golden Land,* the not-so-flattering history of how the elves took over this territory? *That* Elise Sasini?"

Cal flicked a floating tendril of white hair out of his eyes and answered smugly, "Yes. She's *my* mate."

Kaz looked like he almost didn't believe him. "How the fuck did you swing that one?"

"She wanted to write a book about me," he answered, lips curling into a rare smile. "Apparently, she's wanted to do it all her life. You should see her home. It's covered in pictures of my fog." And she'd been tickled to learn that at least a handful of those photos actually *did* have Cal in them, though no one but him would ever know it. "She figured out that I visit the Aerie sometimes, so she booked a pilgrim's stay and summoned me."

"You still go to the Aerie? What for?" A deep frown settled into the grooves of Kaz's mouth and forehead. "Do you need help? I thought we figured out how to get you things when you need them, Cal."

He shrugged, not meeting his friend's searching gaze. Instead, he looked at the rows and rows of bottles behind the bar when he answered, "I don't really know why I go there, after everything. Sometimes I just need something familiar." He cleared his throat. "But I don't have any reason to go there anymore. I have a home now."

"With Elise?"

Cal's smile crept back onto his face. "Yes."

"Good," Kaz grunted. "Better a story-sniffing writer than the assholes who tried to brainwash you."

"Agreed. Elise is a much nicer alternative." He had trouble imagining anyone better, if he were being honest. "And our deal was painless. She wanted to write a book about me and I wanted to know what it was like to have a mate. Simple."

Kaz stared at him for several long, silent seconds before he said, "...Uh-huh?"

"What? Why are you looking at me like that?"

"S'nothing." Kaz took a long pull from his beer. His eyebrows seemed to have permanently adhered themselves closer to his hairline. "Just... ah, that's quite the deal you made, fog man. I'm surprised she went for it."

Cal clenched his jaw and fought off the urge to snap at his friend. "Why? Because I'm a murderer?"

"No, you prissy fuck, because there's no *pretending* to be mates. You either are or you aren't. Trying to fake it is a recipe for disaster and I'm willing to bet she knows that." He eyed Cal warily. "I'm guessing you've been on some dates? Met up to talk about the book, maybe? She probably let you hold her hand or something, right? And now you're head over heels for the first woman to—"

"No," he snapped, "it's not like that."

Kaz's dismissive tone sent a roar of anger through Cal. He hated the way he alluded to their relationship like it was some passing fancy, or like Elise was merely indulging him. It was more than that. Cal felt it in every damn cell of his body.

"She brought me to her home, and when she learned that people usually only want to take advantage of me, she tried to back out. She said she didn't want to hurt me." Even now, weeks later, he felt a stab of panic at the thought. "I wouldn't let her back out."

"Why? Sounds like she has a bit of good sense."

Cal curled his hands into fists on his thighs. "Because she's my mate. I don't care if she uses me. She's mine. I wasn't going to give her up."

"Uh-huh. And how'd she take that?"

He lifted his chin. This part, at least, he knew he got right. "She *kissed* me."

Kaz looked both impressed and dismayed. "Yeah? And after?"

"What do you mean *after?*"

"I mean what happened after that? Has she kept to the deal? Are you still seeing her?" Kaz blew out a breath. "And what *exactly* were the terms of that deal you made?"

Cal leaned an elbow on the bar top and smiled. "Of course I'm still seeing her. We've been living together for three weeks. That was the deal."

The orc sputtered, choking on a gulp of his disgusting beverage. When he'd cleared his airways enough to speak, he wheezed, "Wait, you're *living* with her? She let you into her nest?"

"Yes." Cal took in Kaz's stunned expression with a pinch of unease. "Why? Does that mean something?"

It meant something to *him* to be allowed into her home, but that was because he'd never set foot in one before. It never occurred to him that it might mean something to her, too.

Kaz let out a huff that was somehow both disbelieving and amused. "I mean, if she were orcish it would mean a fuckload, but I'm guessing she's not, if you're here complaining about not being permanently mated. An orcish woman doesn't let *anyone* into her nest except her mate and babies. Not even family." His eyebrows pinched thoughtfully as he swirled the last of his beer around the bottom of his bottle. "Still, though— *Living* with a woman. Yeah, that's..." His eyes crinkled at the corners. "That's a different thing, fog man. What else have you done?"

"We spend most of our time together." Except for when he felt the itch to be out of his skin and his duty to watch the city came up, they were inseparable. Where she went, he did. "We go to the beach. Sometimes she likes to dance with me. We watch entertainment feeds and cook together. I met her parents."

Kaz put his bottle down on the bar with enough force to send a crack through the glass. "Well fuck me, you should have led with that!"

"Why?"

"Goddess help me." Kaz released his beer long enough to rub the heels of both hands into his eyes. "Cal, if you move in with a woman *and* she takes you to see her parents *and* you spend all your time together, you aren't temporary anything. You're *mated.*"

"No," he pressed, heart beating faster, "she's sticking to the deal. She hasn't said anything about staying together after she finishes the book. In fact, tonight she tried to *end* things."

"Did she say why?"

Cal's stomach curdled when he remembered the stark look on her face, the marrow-deep fear he felt when he thought she was sending him away. His voice was hushed and just a little raw when he explained, "I got angry with her for not introducing me to her parents as her mate. She said she was worried about putting pressure on me, that what we were doing was hurting me, and asked me if I'd like to end things."

Kaz's sharp-eyed gaze lingered on Cal's pained expression. "Fog man… she asked *you* if you wanted to end things. She didn't say *she* wanted to."

"She wouldn't have said it if she didn't want it!"

Kaz rolled his eyes. "Don't be a dipshit. She was trying to take care of you. My bet is she knows this is your first relationship and is working overtime trying to make sure you never feel overwhelmed or cornered. *Especially* if you've already moved in together, for Glory's sake."

"But—"

"No buts!" Kaz snagged his cracked beer bottle and pointed an accusatory finger at him all in one movement. "I don't know shit about mating, but I know plenty about women. I was raised by a damn clutch of them. That does *not* sound like a woman running from commitment to me, Cal." He made a swirling motion with his finger. "Now tell me what happened next. What did she do when you said no?"

Cal ran a hand through the length of his hair and leaned

slightly away, his throat bobbing with a hard swallow. Gods, the memory of her hot mouth and soft, sure hands made him hard all over again. "She... ah... We didn't talk much after that."

"D'you fuck?"

"I'm not answering that." Cal wasn't particularly modest or prudish, but he *was* possessive. He had no intention of sharing their most private, sacred moments with anyone other than his mate.

Kaz laughed and shook his head. "I'm going to go ahead and take that as a yes. And if not, then you got close." He finished off his beer with a long, drawn out sigh. Eyes slanting toward Cal, he announced, "Congrats, fog man. You're mated. Now get the fuck out of this shitty bar and go home."

Cal's chest seized, hope wrapping around his heart like a vice. Still, he needed to be sure. He couldn't risk messing things up any more than he already had. Living without Elise was not an option.

"How do you know she wants to keep me?" he pressed, hands flattening against the sticky bar. "How do you know it's not just the deal?"

Kaz groaned and rolled his shoulders. "Let's see... Did your deal specify that she spend all her time with you?"

"Not exactly, no." He demanded they see each other often, but it was true that his wording was vague. If she'd wanted to, she could have spent far less time with him than she did and he probably wouldn't have known enough to complain. Without knowing her routine or responsibilities, any number of excuses would have simply flown over his head.

"And did your deal specify that she introduce you to her parents?"

"No."

Kaz narrowed his eyes. "Did it specify that she provide sexual favors?"

"No," he gritted out. "I told her that's not what I meant."

Even *he* knew he didn't want sex from someone fundamentally unwilling, even if it was part of a deal she agreed to.

"So..." Kaz began to tick points off on his clawed fingers. "You moved in with her. You're having a sexual relationship with her. You spend all your time together. She introduced you to her parents. When you got upset, she offered you an out, but didn't take one herself." He wiggled his fingers. "You're mated, man."

It was suddenly hard to keep his physical form together. Cal nearly vibrated with excitement, with the urgency to fly across the city and back to the willing arms of his mate.

"How do I know it's permanent?" he rasped.

"Well, I guess you'll just have to ask her," Kaz answered. "Women are all about being *asked,* Cal. They are way more forgiving of a stupid question than an assumption. Don't ever work on assumptions. That way lies sharp claws, poisoned coffee, and nights on the couch."

A cold, crawling fear made its way into his exhilaration. "What if she says she doesn't want me?"

Kaz shrugged. "Then you keep trying until she sends you away. Simple."

Simple. Cal had begun to hate the word. Nothing about his relationship with Elise had been simple.

It was worth it, though. He knew that the moment she let him into her life, and he'd clung onto the deal because he was terrified of letting her go. But Kaz was right. He had to trust Elise to give him the truth when he asked for it. So far, she'd never given him any reason to believe she wouldn't.

Kaz's heavy hand landed on Cal's shoulder. Giving him a hard shove, the orc said, "*Go,* Cal. You've got a mate waiting for you."

He stood up from his bar stool on unsteady legs, his heartbeat a thundering rhythm in his ears. He thought of all the intimate moments they'd shared; how she fell asleep with her head in his lap and how she kissed him whenever he came home from his vigil. He thought of her magic coursing through his fog and the way she brought him into her family's home, wreathed in smiles. He thought of her tears when he told her his story and the long, hot looks she gave him when she thought he wasn't looking.

Gods, was he fucking *blind?*

I have a mate.

I have a mate waiting for me.

Suddenly, nothing else mattered. He needed to be with her. He needed to know, with no hint of doubt, that they were not going to end now or any time in the future. He needed his mate like he needed *air.*

In an instant, Cal dematerialized. The bar's other patrons exclaimed with surprise or consternation as the space was suddenly filled with thick, rolling fog. Kaz's voice rose above the din as he cursed. "Fucking— Damn it, Cal, you can't just drop your clothes in the middle of the bar!"

If he had shoulders, Cal would have shrugged. He didn't give a shit about his clothes. All that mattered was his mate, and she wasn't in *The Broken Tooth.* She was waiting for him at home.

He would be damned if he made her wait a moment longer.

Chapter Seventeen

FROM THE DESK OF ELISE SASINI, A PAGE FROM HER NOTEBOOK DATED FEBRUARY 15th 2045:

Reasons to spend the rest of my life with Cal:

1. I love him

2. He's the most beautiful man in the world, bar none

3. I really *love him*

4. He's an insanely powerful elemental whose magic meshes with mine like we're a damn PB and J.

5. I don't think I can live without him

Reasons to not spend the rest of my life with Cal:

[PAGE IS BLANK]

Chapter Eighteen

Elise couldn't sleep. She knew that there was no reason to stay up and wait for Cal. He would be home when it suited him, as he always was, but her mind refused to turn off.

What was he doing? Was he safe? Did he regret what they'd done in the annex?

She shifted restlessly in her bed. Fisting a handful of her blankets, she turned on her side and stared out at the sea of lights visible through her bedroom window — unlocked, just in case he decided to blow in sometime during the night.

Anxiety mingled with a dreadful, unfulfilled arousal.

Gods, but she loved the taste of him. Elise had always been a sexual being, but sex with Cal was *different.* Everything he did — every little sound, every shift of his muscles, every involuntary, stuttering breath — thrilled her to the core. He made her feel powerful and in control. There was nothing more intoxicating than guiding him through his first sexual experiences.

The ache between her legs hadn't diminished even after the explosion. It persisted as she helped her mother clean up the living room and gave a faceless Patrol officer her statement. It didn't let up even after she got home and took a cleansing shower.

It was a good sort of ache, of course, but Elise couldn't shake the concern that she overwhelmed Cal. They'd fought and then he had what she was astonished to learn was his first orgasm. Neither were followed up with a talk or a check-in to make sure he was all right.

Is that why he left?

Elise rolled over again. Her eyes stung. Instead of staring at her closet and wall of framed articles, she forced herself to try and sleep.

But the worries came at her from all sides, robbing her of rest.

She pictured Cal out there, dematerialized and enmeshed in fog as he drifted over the water. Was he angry at her? Did he feel guilt or shame for what he'd done? She knew he still struggled with much of what Loft's acolytes tried to indoctrinate him with. Did he think they'd done something wrong?

Whatever it was that bothered him, she was certain they could work through it. The problem was that he had to *be* there to do that.

Elise curled her legs closer to her chest, a bloom of hurt taking root in her heart. She hated the idea that he might be out there confused and hurt and alone. She hated being without him. For all that he'd never slept in her bed, she felt it was cold and barren without him.

Part of loving Cal was understanding that he did not just belong to her. No matter what her possessiveness said, he was a force of nature. He was *wild.* He could not be held in one place any more than he could stay in his physical form indefinitely. He had to roam because it was his nature. He had to do his vigil because it was his duty.

She understood this. As a weather witch with an unbridled awe for the wildness of the world, she even respected it.

But the part of her that was a woman in love had to come to terms with the fact that he would not always be home at night. He would never sleep beside her, nor would he take her out to dinner and a show.

She didn't begrudge him those things. Cal was who he was.

Elise wouldn't want him any other way. Part of loving someone was trusting them to come back to you — even when they were the physical embodiment of something as ephemeral as *fog*. If she wanted a boring, five-in-the-evening-to-eight-in-the-morning kind of guy, she could have one.

Cal spoke to her soul. She didn't and never would want anyone like she wanted him. But that didn't mean she couldn't worry.

It was an exhausting night. First, the nerves that came with introducing Cal to her parents. Then their fight. Then the rush of going down on him for the first time. *Then* the explosion. Elise felt like she'd lived a year of her life in less than eight hours.

Sleep pulled her down, though her worries fought it every step of the way.

~

FROM THE DESK OF ELISE SASINI, AN EXCERPT FROM THE MANUSCRIPT *THE SHROUDED CITY:*

I've loved before. My first boyfriend was Jeremy Ackerman, a wolf shifter, in the fifth grade. I loved him.

I dated Dan, a fellow journalism student, for three years. I loved him, too. I've loved strangers on the m-lev and I've loved men who never loved me back.

I've loved before, but I've never loved like I love Cal.

Maybe it's something base and fundamental in our magic that draws us together. Maybe it's just chemistry. Maybe it's whatever unseen hand that people like to believe guides these things. I don't know.

All I know is that Cal is wild, and beautiful, and strange, and sometimes hard to get along with. He is broken and he is proud and he is carrying scars I can't even see. Every day I look at him and I see a deep, dark pool of secrets desperately trying to get out — and I see a man who wants to be held and yet does not have the words necessary to say so.

I see my whole future in a single, mercurial being, and if the gods truly exist, then only they can appreciate the scope of my devotion to him.

Chapter Nineteen

The feeling of cool air on her arms and face roused her from a fitful dose, but it was the feeling of chilly hands that *really* woke her.

Her eyes popped open. Elise sat up with a start, but it took her a few confused moments to understand what she was seeing. Fog was everywhere. Even her furniture seemed to have disappeared under the waves of pillowy white that poured in through her open window. Only the faint green glow of the emergency light by the bottom of her bedroom door managed to break through the cloud of condensed moisture. Magic skated over her skin, adding to the otherworldly sense of disorientation.

"Cal?" she whispered, seeking out his form beneath the swirling water vapor. Elise braced her weight on one elbow and squinted into the strange, shifting mass in the darkness of her bedroom. Relief quickly bled into her confusion.

Cool hands framed her face. In the span of a few heartbeats, he melted out of the fog. Elise didn't think she would ever tire of seeing the miracle of his existence recreated every single time he materialized in front of her.

One moment there was only the sense of him in the mist; the next water and air and magic compressed to make a living, breathing man so beautiful she sometimes wondered if he was truly real.

Cal's expression, when it appeared, was intense. His brows were drawn tight over his black eyes; his soft lips pressed thin. The hands cupping her face were gentle but firm, unyielding, and the weight of his body settling on top of hers was both comfortable and erotic. Elise would have enjoyed it more if the look on his face didn't send a dizzying sense of dread through every nerve.

She cupped one of his hands with her own and tried to swallow the lump in her throat. "What's wrong?"

Was this it? Was he here to tell her he was done with whatever their relationship was?

Gods, let it be anything but that. Elise would have taken almost anything rather than Cal finally deciding to end his experiment in intimacy with her.

His voice was its usual low murmur, but there was a distinct raw edge to it that raised her hackles when he said, "I need to ask you a question."

Slowly scooting up into a sitting position, she scanned his face for any hint of what was bothering him. Nothing in his expression screamed that he was upset over what happened in the annex, but Cal's moods were mercurial. She never really knew what was going on just below the surface, and it was something that thrilled her. He was full of surprises.

Elise normally appreciated that about him, but not this time.

Pressing his hand more firmly into her cheek, she answered, "Ask me whatever you want, baby."

Cal shifted in front of her, though the fog made it hard to see exactly what he was doing. It moved restlessly around the room to swirl in dense eddies. Usually that meant he was agitated, and that knowledge only made Elise's stomach drop even further.

Please don't let this be it. Already her eyes had begun to water. The moment he actually said the words, she feared the dam would break completely.

His hands slid down from her cheeks to cup her neck. Goosebumps prickled her skin. Cal ran much cooler than she did, and when he touched her, it felt like the kiss of sweet, fresh water on overheated skin.

Firming his chin into a stubborn angle, he asked, "Are we permanent?"

Bracing herself for the worst, Elise could only blink, stunned. "I... what?"

In the dark, with the fog blocking most of the reflected light of the city, Cal's eyes were too unbroken pools of black ink. They might have looked menacing, if only she didn't know exactly how much he gave of himself every single day to every person in their ignorant city — if only she didn't love him so damn much.

Cal pressed closer, until he was practically straddling her. "Are we *permanent?*"

Her heartbeat picked up its pace. She wanted to tell him *yes,* of course they were permanent, but Elise knew that not everything was as it seemed with Cal. His question could come from the desire to *make* them permanent, or it could just as easily spring from a desire to get as far away from commitment as possible.

Not that I really think Cal's terrified of commitment, she thought, recalling his visceral fear and anger in the annex, *but you never know. Someone like Cal could change their mind in a heartbeat.*

He was, after all, *weather.* One moment he could be as placid as a sunny day, and the next he could be a raging storm. Respecting him, *loving* him, meant understanding the nature of his being, so Elise knew she had to forgo any assumptions. Like always, she needed to be careful.

"Explain, please," she said. Reaching out to smooth her hands down his naked chest, she added, "Tell me what you mean by *permanent.*"

Cal scowled impatiently. "I spoke to Kaz tonight and he told me we are already mates, but if I wanted to be sure that we are mates *forever,* I needed to ask you. So I'm asking you."

"Wait— Kaz? Who's Kaz? Is that your friend?" He'd mentioned having a friend a few times, but Cal had never given her a name before. Something about it sounded familiar, though she couldn't put her finger on why.

Making an impatient sound in the back of his throat, Cal leaned in until he was nearly nose to nose with her. His breath washed over her face in cool, sweet-scented puffs. "Don't think about Kaz. Think about me. Are we permanent mates?"

Elise grappled with her answer, but couldn't come up with anything better than, "Do you *want* to be?"

Cal reared back, his expression outraged. "Do I *want* to be? You're *my* witch. Of course that's what I want!"

She stared up at him, lips parted with surprise. No, she couldn't just take that at face value. Cal didn't necessarily understand what he was saying, what he was *asking* for. How could he really know? He'd only been in a relationship for three weeks. She at least had the experience of being with other people around which she could frame her feelings for him. Cal didn't have that luxury.

When she could find her voice, she rasped, "Cal, I know you think that's what you want, but you haven't had enough time—"

"Do *not* say that I can't know what I want because I'm inexperienced," he growled. "I know now that you've been cautious with me, taking care of me. I don't need that. I just need to know that you want me as much as I want you."

Chapter Twenty

Elise's throat felt scraped raw. Her heart beat so fast and hard, it felt like it might break through the cage of her ribs, leaving nothing but splinters behind. This was what she wanted, but she still warred with herself.

Gods, she wanted to love this man until the breath left her body for the last time, but the fear of somehow taking a natural choice from him was excruciating.

Cal deserved a life and choices. He deserved every experience, every joy, but those things were stolen from him. To count herself as one of the many who simply *took* from him without regard for what was healthy or right made her feel sick to her stomach.

And yet, when the seconds dragged by without her response, Elise realized something else: By not being honest with him, *she was doing exactly that.*

Cal's expression had begun to drain of its intensity, leaving nothing but a stark, beautiful mask. There was nothing left of his vibrant, difficult personality — just staggering pain. Even his fog went still as he took her silence for a rejection.

He released her neck with a quick, jerky movement and recoiled, the edges of his form already fading from view as he retreated into the safety of his other form.

"No, Cal!" Elise lunged, freeing herself from her tangled blankets to tackle him back onto the bed. She knew instinctively that if she let him dematerialize and drift back out of her window, she would never see him again.

And that wasn't a *fucking* option.

"No, no," she said, straddling his waist. Cal's hands snapped up to cup her backside as she leaned down. Her hair fell in a messy blonde curtain around their heads when she whispered against his stiff lips, "I want you, Cal. I don't want to go a day of my life without seeing you. I want to kiss you and hold you and deal with your brooding for the rest of my life. I've known it since the day you walked into my apartment."

Cal's fingers flexed, pressing hard against soft skin covered in thin sleep shorts. His voice was a raw murmur when he asked, "The deal?"

"I threw it out of my head that same day." She pressed her hands to his naked chest. His heartbeat was just as fast as hers, a thunderous rhythm against her palm. Elise touched her forehead to his and whispered, "All I cared about was keeping you around, Cal. I don't even care about the book."

"But..." She could feel his brow crinkle. "I saw you writing."

She felt herself flush. "Well, it would have been weird if I didn't at least *pretend* to write something, wouldn't it?"

Cal's hands slid down her thighs. His palms left her shorts to skim down her bare skin, sending a low pulse of heat through her body. "So you didn't actually write anything down?"

"No, I wrote something," she amended, sitting up a little so she could get a good look at his face. Cal was spread out beneath her, his mane of white hair haloed around his aquiline face and his eyes half-lidded. His fingertips dug into the soft flesh of her thighs, dimpling her skin.

Perhaps sensing her hesitancy, he demanded, "Tell me what you wrote."

Elise licked her lips and tried very hard not to be distracted by the beautifully naked man lying beneath her. "I... It's more of a love letter, if I'm being honest. I wrote down what you told me, but I also wrote a lot about... well, about how I feel. About what I think of you. All of it."

Cal stared up at her with a familiar, hungry expression. "And how do you feel?"

She tried to shake off the bizarrely sentimental urge to cry. Elise wasn't normally a weepy sort of person, but the relief she felt was so intense, it was like her body needed some cathartic release to process it all.

In a watery voice, she answered, "I'm stupidly in love with you, Cal."

Infuriatingly, all he said was, "So... we're permanent."

It was her turn to scowl. Sitting back so she could look down her nose at him, she muttered, "I sure *hope* so, or else I'm going to be very upset, very soon."

He was still beneath her for several awful seconds before a heartstopping smile broke out across his face. Cal so rarely smiled in earnest, but when he did, it damn near knocked Elise's world sideways.

Nodding to himself and looking very pleased, he said, "Kaz was right. Stupid questions *are* better."

A laugh bubbled up and out of her throat. "*What?*"

Cal slid his hands back up to curl around her waist. His eyes gleamed when he asked, "If you love me and we're mates, does that mean you're not going to be careful anymore?"

Elise sucked in a sharp breath when he gently pushed her down onto the swiftly hardening erection trapped between them. Desire, pushed back by worry, came roaring back in an instant. She wanted nothing more than to chase away the ache with a quick strip and slow, sensual ride.

Still, she had to ask, "Are you sure, baby? That's a big step."

"Will it be like the annex?" His voice was rough as he slowly began to move her hips back and forth, dragging her against him in a torturous rhythm.

Elise felt him through the damp seam of her sleep shorts and bit back a moan. "Better," she breathed. "It'll be better."

She watched, transfixed, as the muscles of Cal's lean stomach bunched and released with every slow stroke against her. "Show me," he demanded. "I want *everything,* witch."

Finally.

There would be no more holding back. No more tip-toeing. No more worry. Cal wanted everything, and Elise was desperate to give it to him.

Grasping the hem of her sleep shirt, she didn't hesitate to tear it up and over her head. It landed in a heap somewhere on the floor, though she couldn't see where through the dense, roiling layer of fog obscuring everything except Cal.

The presence of his fog gave an already intimate act an even more private, sacred feeling. In this moment, there really was nothing except the two of them and their combined, complimentary magic. It filled the room with the sharp, metallic scent of power and fresh water — blood and life and weather's rage and deep, scalding desire.

It took her only a moment to sit up and wiggle her way out of her sleep shorts, but she was breathing hard by the time she threw her leg back over his waist and settled her weight down. They both groaned when her liquid heat finally met his cool skin. Cal gasped — the sweetest godsdamned sound she ever heard — and tossed his head back against the mattress.

"Tell me if you want to stop," she firmly instructed him. "If it's uncomfortable or too much, just say—"

"Elise," he hissed, hips kicking up to grind against her core. "I'm going to die if you don't do *something."*

She laughed, but didn't argue. How could she? Elise felt exactly the same way.

The memory of his taste on her tongue, the way he'd unraveled above her as she gave him pleasure like he'd never known it, practically lit her on fire.

Seeing such a powerful being lie prone beneath her, desperate for the relief she could provide, made her *explode.*

Elise braced her palms on the mattress by his ears and leaned down to kiss him long and hard, her hips moving in slow circles above him. He made a needy noise and rocked his hips to match her rhythm as his tongue snaked out to meet hers.

Never would she get bored of kissing Cal. He tasted like a storm, like everything that called to the soul of a weather witch. Even their magic meshed as they moved together, sliding against one another in a sensual dance.

Cool, dry hands slid up her sides to explore the soft skin of her stomach, her ribs, her back, and her breasts. When he stopped there, apparently fascinated by her stiff nipples, Elise broke the kiss to sit back and let him follow his instincts.

"You're so warm and soft," he breathed, awed, as he gently rolled her nipples between his fingertips. Elise sucked in deep breath as streaks of pleasure flashed down her spine to settle into a deep pool between her thighs. It was only made richer, sweeter, when he asked, "I get to have you forever?"

Taking one of his hands off of her breast, she brought it up to her lips for a slow, reverent kiss. "Yes," she whispered against his palm, "as long as you'll have me."

"Forever, then." His tone was suddenly implacable, hard as granite. Cal's hips canted upward with one hard thrust, as if to make his point. "I want forever with you, Elise. You're *my* mate."

She gasped, back bowing. "Yes, Cal, I am. *Yes.*"

His hand went back to her breast, squeezing gently, as she reached between them to align their bodies. He was thick and hard in her palm. Even in the darkness, she could *just* make out the pearly sheen of his skin. It just wasn't fair. How was it that even his damn *cock* was gorgeous?

"You're mine too," she said, reminding them both as she slowly lowered herself down onto him. It was a tight fit, but the delicious kind that sent a cascade of sparks across every nerve. It was so good, even her toes curled.

All around them, sparks of her magic danced through the fog, lighting up their naked bodies with bursts of pink and teal and bright, saturated yellow.

Cal made a strangled sound and dropped his hands to grip her hips. Every muscle in his body went rigid as she took him all the way to the hilt. She held still, panting, as she adjusted to the perfect fit, the feeling of him soothing that deep, empty ache even as it burned muscles she hadn't used in a while.

"You okay?" she asked, the words barely registering in her own ears.

His fingers flexed hard on her hips as he gave one, then two experimental thrusts upward. The sounds of their skin meeting echoed strangely in the fog, enhancing the feeling of otherworldliness, the profound intimacy of the moment. Pleasure seared away the lingering burn of the stretch as Cal's spine bowed. *"Gods,"* he gritted out, "I'm— Elise!"

"Shh," she soothed. Picking a slow, rocking rhythm, she took one of his hands and guided it between her legs. "Focus on me, baby. Touch me. And don't forget to breathe."

His fingers spasmed, as if touching her sent a shock straight through him, but Cal didn't hesitate to do as she instructed. Slowly, he followed the movement of her hips to rub her clitoris — tentatively at first, then with more confidence as she gave him soft instructions. It wasn't long before a fine sheen of sweat coated her body and her rocking turned into something more urgent.

Cal's chest moved with huge, gulping inhales as he let her ride him, his own hips stuttering beneath her. Elise gripped his shoulders and panted, "Sit up, baby. Sit up. I want to kiss you when I—"

He surged upward and would have sent her toppling over if he didn't have such a tight grip on her waist. Elise let out a bark of laughter as he leaned in close enough to bump their noses together.

"Oh, gods, I love you, you weird fog man," she wheezed, peppering his cheeks and nose and lips with kisses.

Cal smiled against her lips and wrapped his arms around her middle, holding her still as he rocked his hips up and down. "I love you, witch." Cool, wet fog kissed her overheated skin, running along her curves with purpose as he continued, "I am your mate. Permanently."

"Yes, permanently." Elise wiggled back just enough to move. Bracing her knees by his hips, she used the leverage to increase the pace. A coil of pressure and heat tightened, urging her to go faster, to chase the friction building like a fire between them. Cal met her stroke for stroke, though his movements weren't quite so fluid or practiced as hers.

It didn't matter. Sex with Cal was more than pleasurable. It was more than raw physical release. This was like everything good, and fun, and warm, and intense, and new, and thrilling she had ever felt multiplied by the thousands.

This powerful being, an act of elemental wrath made corporeal, was *hers.* Only she would know what he looked like when he came. Only she would give him pleasure. Only she would have complete mastery of his bliss.

Gods be good, it's enough to make any woman lose her mind. She would have laughed, if she had the breath for it. *No wonder love is called Tempest's Madness!*

When Cal's thrusts began to really lose their rhythm, she knew he was close to the edge. Yanking his head down, she fisted his beautiful, wild hair and pressed their lips together in a searing, open-mouthed kiss. He let out a low, broken sound as fog danced across her naked skin — and then swept between them to tease and rub her clitoris when his hand could not, sending her even higher.

I didn't even know he could do *that,* she thought, a split second before Cal came apart beneath her. Tendrils of compressed magic and water lashed at her with erratic, frenzied movements, sending her over the edge with him. Her thighs clenched, holding him there as he gave her everything he possibly could.

When the pleasure ebbed, they were both left sagging and

boneless on her bed. Cal kept his arms around her, but dropped his head to nuzzle her neck and shoulder. He mumbled something into her skin, but it was too low for her to catch.

"What was that?" she asked, dazed.

His lips moved against the sweaty skin of her throat when he said, "I'm thanking the gods for bringing me to you."

Elise's heart gave a great, painful lurch. "Yeah?"

"Yeah." He kissed her throat. "You are my everything, witch."

She murmured, "Never thought I'd earnestly thank the gods for anything but orgasms, but I'm gonna say thank you, too. I never want to imagine my life without you, Cal."

"You will never have to." Stroking her hair, he added, "And just so we're clear, I'm *not* broody."

She smothered a laugh by pressing a kiss to the crown of his head. "Mm, if you say so, baby."

Slowly, in fits and starts, they repositioned themselves in her bed. Cal didn't sleep, but there was a drowsy, satisfied look in his eyes that made him content to settle down with her under her sheets. Resting her head on his chest, she listened to the strong sound of his heartbeat as she breathed in the cold, wet air.

She was half asleep when he asked, "Will you let me read your love letter?"

Her smile was so wide, it made her cheeks ache. "Yes," she whispered, kissing his chest. "But only the second draft."

Chapter Twenty-One

FROM THE DESK OF CALAMITY, A NOTE WRITTEN IN AN ANNOTATED FIRST EDITION COPY OF *THE SHROUDED CITY,* BESTSELLING NON-FICTION TITLE AND WINNER OF THE PULITZER PRIZE - BIOGRAPHY:

Pg. 342

I am in awe of you, my mate. Every day I love you more than the day before, and every day I learn something new and precious about you.

Pg. 343

I THOUGHT WE AGREED YOU'D STOP CALLING ME BROODY.

EPILOGUE

OCTOBER 2047 - SAN FRANCISCO, THE ELVISH PROTECTORATE

CAL WOULD NEVER LIKE PUBLICITY. HE DIDN'T CARE for nosy people trying to track him down, or the throngs of folks who, for some time after *The Shrouded City's* publication, gathered on the beaches to try and catch a glimpse of him. He hadn't changed his mind about his anonymity, nor his general dislike for most people.

It was a strange thing, knowing that so many strangers read his story and felt, to no small degree, as though they *knew* him. He couldn't say he was really a fan of that.

What made it all worth it, though, was the absolute certainty he had in his claim on Elise. While he didn't enjoy the fresh scrutiny the book brought him, Cal pushed his mate to publish it on the grounds that it would show the entire world that they belonged to one another.

Not that they *needed* it, really, but Cal erred on the side of caution. He didn't feel he deserved his mate's devotion, but he was a jealous creature. If he was lucky enough to call her his, then he wanted every single being in the world to know about it.

Cal didn't have much experience in gauging the success or failure of books, but even he knew the furor around *The Shrouded City* was abnormal. The thing had only been out for a month, but it was all anyone wanted to talk about.

When he drifted past bookshop windows, he saw piles of it stacked waist-high. When a news feed alert came in on Elise's Met, it was almost always something about the book. When he was home with her, he listened to call after call, interview after interview, and made absolutely certain he was nowhere near a camera.

The only reviews and articles he cared about were the ones that gushed over their whirlwind love story — a turn of phrase that tickled Elise immensely. Everything else he ignored. Cal didn't care about the money that came in, or the upswell in public affection for him. When Kaz tried to coerce him into meeting with the Solbourne PR team, a group particularly interested in the chapters dedicated to his imprisonment and how they reflected on the current regime, he promptly dematerialized.

Cal didn't care about anything other than the public's recognition of his relationship. If Elise got acclaim for the book on top of that, then he was perfectly content to ignore the garbage that came with being suddenly *beloved* by millions of people.

"What put that scowl on your face?" Elise asked as soon as he materialized in their living room. She was curled up on the couch, a throw blanket tossed over her legs and her tablet clutched in one hand. There was a small, stemless glass of red wine in the other.

Cal closed the window with a flick of his fingers before he prowled over to his mate. When he left her in the afternoon, she'd been dolled up for a video interview, but now she was relaxed, her face clean and her thick blonde hair piled into a wispy bun. Bare toes peeked out from under the blanket.

Feeling his tension ease at the sight of her, relaxed and waiting for him, Cal grumbled, "They brought *signs* this time."

Elise snorted. Her eyes glittered with humor at his expense. "You *have* to tell me what they said!"

"No, I do not," he tartly replied, making his way over to the couch. Elise laughed and scooted to the far end, making plenty of room for him to lay down and put his head in her lap.

He still couldn't sleep, but he had grown very fond of lounging, so they upgraded their furniture. The two-seater couch changed to a behemoth that took up most of their living room, while their bed went from a queen to a California king. Cal was what Elise playfully called "a sprawler".

Not that she truly seemed to mind, of course. His mate was always ready to receive him with open arms. When he returned from his vigil, she enjoyed hearing about all that he'd done and seen in the city, while he hungrily devoured any new tidbit she offered him — how her day was, what she wrote, what strange thing had captured her formidable interest that day.

Always, she made sure to offer him contact. Rarely more than a moment went by when she was not stroking his hair or curled under his arm. Even when she cooked, Elise would make a point to brush her fingers over his skin whenever she drifted by him. Never once did she forget that he was once starved for affection, and every moment of every day she sought to shower him with it.

In return, he basked in her glow and did everything he could to encourage her rampant curiosity. Together, they explored every corner of the city and its archives. He plucked the juiciest bits from his long memory for her and hovered nearby whenever she lost herself in writing. He loved her and he was in awe of her. Cal saw it as his job to remind her just how extraordinary she was every day, lest she forget.

"Where were they this time?" she asked, setting her wine down on the edge of the small coffee table. A stack of battered notebooks took up most of the space. With her hand free, she gently nudged him until he lay in the perfect position for her to run her fingers through his long, unruly hair.

Cal closed his eyes, savoring the feeling of her blunt nails scraping gently against his scalp, and cupped her kneecap with one possessive hand. There was a small flare of magic as his fog seeped into the air, wrapping with equal possessiveness around the rest of her.

He could hardly fathom the life he lived before her, before *this.* Really, it didn't seem like much of a life at all.

"They were on the bridge," he complained. "About forty people, all of them waving signs. What in the world did they expect me to do with that? Stop to take photos?"

"Maybe they just wanted to let you know they appreciate everything you do for the city, baby."

"Yeah, well, they could be quieter about it," he grumbled.

"Poor fog man," she cooed, patting his head. "It's so hard being beloved, isn't it?"

Cal hid his smile in the blanket covering her thigh. Giving her knee a quick squeeze, he said, "Hush. This is all your fault."

"My fault? I'll remind you that *I* was the one who said we shouldn't publish the book." It was her turn to give his ear a tiny pinch. "You were the one who pushed, remember?"

"Yes, because I wanted everyone to know how much you loved me," he smugly replied. Turning his head, he looked up and found her grinning down at him, the skin around her hazel eyes crinkling. Cal lifted a hand to stroke the freckles on her cheek, a sigh of contentment on his lips. "Read that part to me again," he playfully demanded. "You know the one."

Elise blushed, as she always did when he asked her to read to him. "Didn't we just read that bit last night?"

"Yes. I want to hear it again."

It didn't matter that he'd read the book a dozen times, nor that she read excerpts from it whenever he asked her to. Cal would never get tired of seeing the words, *hearing* them. And for all that Elise blushed and grumbled, he saw the smile that tugged her full lips up and knew that she enjoyed it as much as he did.

"Fine," she sighed, using her thumb to scroll through the files on her tablet. When she found the right one, she settled her free hand on his brow and began, *"He is* Calamity. *He is a force of nature more powerful and vast than our government would comfortably admit. He is all-consuming. He is an act of godly wrath made flesh, and by some miracle, he has chosen to be kind to us."*

Cal closed his eyes. His chest felt too small to hold in everything he felt for her, how grateful he was to be hers. All he could do was wrap his arms around her middle, holding her tight, in the vain hope that it could express even some small amount of his love for her.

Elise's voice was soft and sure when she continued, "*He is Calamity. He is mine. The first time Cal kissed me, I knew it like I knew my magic, my heart, my hands. The kind of knowing that is instinctive and soulful even when it is new and terrifying."* She caressed his cheek with the backs of her fingers, her voice dropping to a whisper. *"He is mine and I am his. Forever."*

THE END

Chapter one of Grim's Delight

UNKNOWN NUMBER

Hello, pet

who is this

Tell me who you think it is

someone I definitely didn't give my number to

You would've. Sadly I didn't have time to convince you when we met. You ran off before I had the chance

when was that

also, doubtful

We met at the lush

I meet a lot of people at the bar. I probably won't remember you

You'd remember me.

then why don't you jog my memory

You encounter a lot of body bags in your line of work, pretty girl?

JULY 2048 - SAN FRANCISCO, THE ELVISH PROTECTORATE

SHE KNEW IT'D BE A SHIT NIGHT.

Dahlia McKnight didn't like to think of herself as superstitious. She much preferred the term *intuitive.* The universe moved in predictable patterns. More than once, her survival had depended on being able to read the signs all around her.

That was why, when she woke up to no message notification, a knot of dread tied itself around the base of her spine and held fast.

It wasn't an unusual occasion, necessarily. There were long stretches — weeks, months — where she heard nothing at all. But something about *this* evening felt off.

It was another bad sign when she stepped into her tiny cubicle of a shower to become the unsuspecting victim of a spray of frigid water. Her yelp was loud enough to draw the attention of her closest neighbor. Though that wasn't hard, considering their bathroom windows faced one another with only a foot gap between them.

"If you trip and die in the shower, I'll put panties on you before I call Patrol," Cecilia informed her, as chipper and helpful as always.

Dahlia danced out of the shower, her teeth clacking, and snatched a towel off the hook. She didn't care if Cecilia saw her tits — they'd compared sizes when they were thirteen and had synced periods since the damn things started — but she needed the warmth. It didn't matter how warm the weather got. Their apartment building was always freezing.

Kneeling on the toilet, Dahlia pushed the window open a bit more and stuck her head into the strange, dark gap between their apartments. Her best friend's perfume drifted in the musty air.

"My hot water is out again," she groused.

It only took a second for Cecilia's face to appear in her open window. Holding a curling iron in one hand, she pushed up her window with the other. "You wanna use mine? Should be a little bit of warm water left." She paused to squint her dark eyes speculatively. "Wait, are you working tonight? I thought you were off."

"I swapped with Alexa. There's a VIP thing tonight, so I said yes."

"Oh, big tips." Cecilia jammed her thumb over her shoulder. "You don't have a lot of time before opening, but you wanna use my shower?"

Dahlia shook her head and was immediately annoyed by the situation all over again when she felt how only half her hair was wet. She didn't want to talk about how she'd spent half her getting ready time staring at her phone, waiting for her boogeyman to make himself known.

"It's fine. I just wanted to inform you that today is cursed. I can feel it."

Cecilia nodded solemnly. A little bit of the sincerity of the gesture was ruined when she began curling her hair again, but Dahlia could allow it. "That sucks. I have a date in a couple hours. You think I should cancel?"

"It's worth considering."

"Noted. If I get murdered, you get custody of Oyster."

Dahlia wrinkled her nose as she climbed off the toilet. The salvage operation on her hair and makeup had to start soon or she'd really be up Shit Creek. "I so don't want your dead cat, Cece."

"It's not about what you want," she called back. "It's about familial responsibility, Dahlia! You have to take care of Oyster, discreetly dispose of my sex toys, and for the love of the gods, pick a cute picture of me for them to put on the news feeds. None of that senior photo or embarrassing selfie crap."

Yelling over the roar of her hair dryer, Dahlia complained, "I thought we both agreed I'd die first!"

"That was before you stopped going on dates. I'm on dating apps. My risk of being murdered is much higher than yours now."

"That's dark. Real, but dark." Dahlia tipped her head over and violently blew hot air through her short blonde hair. Scrubbing her fingers through it in a vain attempt to give it a little volume, she argued, "Cece, it's not like you go on dates with criminals. The last guy you had drinks with was a middle school math teacher. And we both work at a vampire bar. I think that makes our mortality risk about equal."

"Ugh, *Jason.*" The sound of hairspray being more than liberally applied came a few seconds before the scent of it drifted across the divide and into Dahlia's bathroom. "I really thought we had fun. I don't understand what happened there."

Personally, Dahlia didn't understand it either. She didn't date because she wasn't willing to risk the life and limb of some poor schmuck who worked in finance, but Cecilia was a different story.

She'd always been the sweet to Dahlia's tart. The pink to her red. The baby to her brat. They'd been thick as thieves since the first day of kindergarten, and despite having seen every single one of Cecilia's most awkward phases and catastrophic fashion choices over the years, Dahlia still thought she was the most beautiful woman in the world.

And *kind.* Fundamentally. Wholly. In all the ways Dahlia had beaten out of her before she ever got a chance to understand what she'd lost.

Cecilia deserved a gorgeous, doting nerd with obscene amounts of money and a high tolerance for pastels, not the milquetoast jerks who kept disappointing her.

Flipping her hair back, Dahlia switched off her blow dryer and scrambled to throw on a halfway decent face of makeup.

Patting concealer under her eyes, she said, "I hope Jason gets hit by a bus."

"Nooo. Didn't you hear about the substitute teacher shortage in San Francisco's school district? His untimely death would put a strain on our education system. Let's hope he gets hit by an electric scooter instead. He can still go to work with a broken leg."

Dahlia reached for her eyelash curler and bit back the retort that it might be helpful if Jason did have an accident that took him fully out of commission. Her friend had recently finished her teaching certification and was jockeying for one of those open positions.

Meanwhile, Dahlia drowned in coursework as she clawed her way to the finish line of her business degree. If she could've gotten to the finish line of a better job with a well-placed shove off a curb, she would've done it.

"Face?"

"Face."

They both appeared at their respective windows. Cecilia looked as soft and sparkly as always, with her warm brown skin glowing and her hair curled into gentle waves. Glitter caught the light on her eyelids and her lip gloss was just the right shade of purple-pink. With those doe eyes and soft lips, Dahlia was almost tempted to date Cecilia herself.

"You're wasted on men," she said, nodding sagely.

"As are you, my sexy friend." Cecilia disappeared for a moment before she leaned out the window, her arm stretching to pass along a tube of lipstick. "Here. This is my lucky red. Wear it as a good luck talisman tonight."

"Thank yo— Wait, Cece, this is *my* lipstick!"

"That's why it's lucky," she replied, utterly shameless. "It was free!"

Popping the cap off, Dahlia warned her friend's retreating back, "If you die, I'm gonna leave your sex toys out on your bed for your parents to find. That glow-in-the-dark dildo is going under your pillow. Your mother will think you used it as a night light, you animal!"

"I guess you'll just have to die first after all. Have fun at work!"

There was no time to plot a more immediate revenge for the theft. Dahlia raced around her studio, pulling on her skimpy uniform, grabbing her purse, and shrugging on her coat with impressive speed. There were many serious downsides to her apartment being so close to The Lush, the vampire bar she'd worked at for five years, but she forgot every last one of them whenever she ran late.

The sun was just beginning to set when she wheeled into the back entrance, out of breath but exactly on time.

No one paid her any mind as she stuffed her belongings into her locker. Inputting her code into the lock, she resisted the urge to check her phone again. Tonight was a big night with — hopefully — big tips. Even if it wasn't, she tried very hard not to think about how reliant on her boogeyman she'd become over the years.

She didn't *miss* him. And she definitely wasn't stupid enough to worry about him. She was just used to his constant annoyances. That was all.

Dahlia tried to shove him from her mind as she scrubbed her hands and forearms in the sanitation station. Someone had already turned on the music for the night. The thumping beat bled through the thick walls. She'd never liked it much, but it was easy to tune out after so many years of practice.

Drying her hands under the UV light, she quickly donned the long white gloves they were all required to wear. All vampire bars made their staff wear gloves, but the ones the staff at The Lush wore were one part utility and three parts kink. The length added something special to their uniform, Devon said. As if the low neckline, mesh décolletage, and high hemline weren't enough.

Her lips thinned. Working VIP events meant great tips, but it also meant exposure to her boss. She'd never seen anyone as desperate to schmooze with bigwigs as Devon, which was saying something.

She hadn't known very much about vampires before she took the server position at The Lush. Dahlia would admit she was still pretty ignorant about the finer details, but it only took her a few months to pick up on the fact that there was just one thing in the world they valued more than blood.

Status.

The nebulous ideals of prestige and respect ruled the vampire underworld, all the way from the lowest of the low to the highest rung. She'd seen fights break out over the smallest of perceived infractions and heard stomach-turning rumors about what happened to servers who thought they could survive an entanglement with one or more of the deadly predators.

A week after she started, a server named Jackson got into trouble when he tried dating two different vampires at once. One of the women ended up dead, disemboweled in the restroom, and Jackson never showed up to work again.

Despite abundant cautionary tales, some servers took the job explicitly to find a wealthy vampire to attach themselves to, but it was a very dangerous game. More often than not they got used and dumped before a permanent bond was formed, leaving them to deal with venom withdrawal on their own. On the rare occasions they didn't, there was almost always another vampire in the wings, furious that someone they thought was already their property had been snapped up.

She and Cecilia had learned quickly that surviving their job meant keeping their heads down, giving good service, and never letting a vampire get attached. *Head down, tray up,* they said.

Of course, that only worked with the customers. Management was another story.

Devon hadn't always been the boss. His brother, Duke, was in charge when she was hired. He'd been thoroughly disinterested in the job and left the staff — and patrons — alone, for the most part. It was a sad day for them all when Devon took over.

His pale blue eyes found her immediately when she stepped out onto the floor, her silver tray tucked under her arm. Devon looked at all the servers like they were meat, but he reserved a special sort of intensity for her.

She'd really hoped he'd roll in fashionably late and a little drunk, like he sometimes did. But he was bright-eyed and bushy-tailed that evening, dressed in his tightest white button-down and slacks. His pale blond hair was swept behind his ears and his thin silver nose ring gleamed in the neon lights of the bar.

Dahlia really had no idea what look he was going for. The closest thing she could come up with was *boy band member meets mobster* in all the worst possible ways.

Gesturing with his claws for her and two other servers, he flashed his fangs in a way that was probably supposed to be intimidating. She sucked in a deep breath and prayed for patience.

"Good evening," he drawled, gaze taking a leisurely stroll up and down her body before flicking toward the other servers assigned to the VIP rooftop lounge. "We've got some really important guests here tonight, so I don't need to tell you what'll happen if you fuck up, do I? I want the synth flowing all night — no limit. The most expensive stuff we have."

He was somehow more wound up than usual tonight. Urgency practically oozed out of him when he ordered, "Whatever you have to do to make our guests happy, you do it. No questions asked. Clear?"

They all nodded. There were no rookies in their little VIP crew, which meant that they all knew it was best to keep their mouths shut.

Dismissing them as carelessly as he summoned them, Dahlia was relieved to be free. She didn't make it three steps in her black pumps before she felt him breathing down the back of her neck.

"Hold on a minute, Dahlia," he purred. Devon didn't touch her, but he didn't need to. She knew better than to disobey.

Gritting her teeth, she counted her blessings that he was

talking to her in the main bar, where servers and bartenders ran around getting everything ready for opening. "Yes, sir?"

"Stick close to me tonight, okay? I want the prettiest woman by my side." He offered her a slow, sensual smile. It was the same one he'd been giving her for months. Why he still thought it worked on her, she had no idea.

Bracing a hand on the bar behind her, he leaned in as close as he could without touching her. Vampires, like most predators, were picky about scents. But like everything else, they took it to an extreme. A server who smelled like a vampire sold fewer drinks. They hated the scent of each other near their food. It had something to do with the fact that vampire venom was toxic to their own kind, meaning no two people could feed from the same source.

If the bar wanted to sell synth, they needed their servers to smell fresh and unclaimed, which meant Devon had to restrain himself from laying his hands on her.

How long that restraint would last, Dahlia didn't know. Devon had been slowly but surely encroaching on her life since he took over the bar. He texted her at odd hours, demanded to know who she spent her days off with, and she was pretty sure she'd seen him — or one of his men — outside her apartment building more than once.

All the signs pointed to his patience running out. She just hoped it wouldn't happen tonight.

"You know I love having you around," he breathed, too close to her ear, "but I hate seeing you work so hard. When are you going to let me take care of you, baby? If it were up to me, you'd be in my penthouse right now, wanting for nothing."

Her skin crawled. Like all the creeps who'd come before him, he made it sound like he wanted to take care of her, to save her from a life of drudgery and poverty with his sky-high credit limit and mediocre pussy petting. He didn't mention what he'd expect in return: her entire life.

If he'd just been after her blood, she *might* have been able to see the appeal in an arrangement, but when vampires fixed on someone, they never settled for something so simple.

Dahlia had seen a lot of bad relationships, but she didn't need any of their examples to know that letting Devon into her life was a terrible idea. Not that he'd get that far. There was a very real reason she'd stopped dating and it wasn't just her lack of free time.

Devon was an asshole, but she didn't want him dead. Yet.

Putting her tray between them like a shield, she slipped away from the bar. "Doors are open. I better get to the lounge."

Devon let her go with a smug half-smile. "See you there, baby."

Pre-order Grim's Delight now!

YOU GONNA SHOOT ME,
PET?

Read Grim's Delight September 23rd!

A bloody war nears its end.

Felix Amauri is the rightful heir to the most powerful vampire crime family on the continent. After years of taking out challengers to his claim, everything he's fought for is finally within reach — until one sloppy assassination threatens to ruin everything.

To be human is to be prey.

For years, the worst thing Dahlia McKnight could picture was becoming a vampire's toy. She never imagined that she'd witness a brutal assassination, let alone that she'd be turned in the process. One day she's a waitress, the next she's the sole heir to a vicious crime family embroiled in a war of succession and the target of an icy vampire prepared to do anything to take what he's owed.

He needs her for more than just her blood.

Learning to be a vampire is hard enough, but when it's discovered that she can carry another vampire's offspring, nothing will stop Felix from claiming her. If she wants to be more than just his plaything, it'll mean becoming the predator she was born to be.

About the Author

Abigail Kelly is an author-illustrator of alternate histories, love stories, and women with drive. Her work is heavily influenced by both her modest family roots and her passion for history. After nearly a decade as a bookseller at independent bookshops, she still loves putting books in eager hands. Her favorite authors are Shirley Jackson, Yangsze Choo, Ursula K. Le Guin, Kresley Cole, Nalini Singh, and just about anyone who writes about the weird and wonderful. She lives in San Francisco with her dog, Babs, who remains stubbornly illiterate.

Glossary

A full character directory and map can be found at Abigailkkelly.com

Places

United Territories and Allies: What we would consider the continental USA. A loose federation of sovereign states established after the Great War. The UTA capital is United Washington, in the Neutral Zone.

The Elvish Protectorate: Also known as the EVP. Stretches from Oregon to New Mexico. Capital city is San Francisco. Led by the elvish sovereign Theodore Thaddeus Solbourne and Margot Goode.

The Coven Collective: Also known as the Collective. Encompasses Washington state. Capital city is Seattle. Led by a large coalition of witch covens, with Sophie Goode acting as their leader.

The Orclind: Encompasses much of the Midwest. Led by the Iron

Chain, a close-knit government made up of orcish clans and Queen Sigrid Seagrim. Capital city is Boulder.

Shifter Alliance: Takes up a section of the midwest and all of the south. (Unfortunately includes Florida.) Run by a very, very loose alliance of shifter packs from three capital cities — Minneapolis, Oklahoma City, and Atlanta. Unofficial leader is Lee Seymour.

The Draakonriik: Also known as the 'Riik. The second smallest territory, it takes up all of the Great Lakes region and stretches to New York. Led by Taevas Aždaja, the *Isand* (ee-zand) of the dragon clans. Pronounced: *dra-kon-reek*

The Neutral Zone: Also known as the New Zone. Technically it is held by a coalition government consisting of representatives from the UTA, but in reality it is run by a syndicate of feuding vampire families. It is a small strip of land squeezed between the Draakonriik and the Shifter Alliance.

Gods

Light & Darkness: The primordial gods who created all the others. Also known as The Lovers and First Union. Both are generally represented as female.

Loft: God of the sky and creator of flying beings. Twin sibling to Tempest. They know no gender. Also known as the Boundless One.

Tempest: God of the ocean and creator of all water beings. Also known as the Hungry God and the god of love.

Burden: God of the Earth, creator of all beings who live within it — most notably the orcs. Husband of Glory.

Glory: Goddess of sunlight, magic, and creator of elves. Worshipped by witches for giving the gift of magic to humanity.

Blight: God of forested places and disease. He works in partnership with his daughter Grim and shares her dominion over demons and all reviled creatures.

Grim: Goddess of death. Known as the Merciful One and the Brilliant Lady. She is widely beloved.

Craft: God of change, newness, and messengers. Creator of humanity and viewed warily by non-worshippers as the Chaos Maker. They change their gender frequently, but generally is referred to using he/him pronouns.

TERMS

Alpha: a broad term used by many communities generally associated with a leader — either of a small family group, a pack, or even a territory.

Anchor: a vampire's mate. Anchors are carefully chosen and usually longterm-to-permanent arrangements, as they take considerable energy to make/become. A vampire must inject their venom into a host many times before their blood chemistry adjusts such that they become unsuitable for consumption by another vampire and their sleep cycle switches to a nocturnal pattern. At this point, they can can also produce/carry to term a vampiric child. Temporary anchors do exist, although they are relatively rare due to the intense withdrawal symptoms associated with ending the regular venom intake.

Arrant: someone born without m-paths, or the ability to channel and use magic.

Burnout: the colloquial name for the degenerative medical condition caused by excessive magic in humans. Over time magic can damage nerves and brain tissue, which will inevitably result in death if not treated with with development of a witchbond.

Change: an elvish term for a sudden shift into adulthood. This is marked by 5-14 days of "madness", usually triggered by some stressful event around the age of 16-18. The elvish body is flushed with hormones to the point where sudden growth, overwhelming hunger, and aggression take over. Viewed as an incredibly vulnerable time, only immediate kin are charged with the care of their loved ones — which includes isolating them, preventing harm to themselves/others, and feeding them. The change marks the second phase of an elf's life, when they are no longer coddled children but young adults who can accept challenges and family responsibilities. Formal adulthood is attained at 30.

Changeling: a term first used to refer to fey children fostered out to non-fey homes, now more widely used to mean any person raised by people who are not the same beings. *Ex:* A dragon couple raising a human child.

Chosen: the formal term for a dragon's mate. The act of finding a mate is called *Choosing,* and is considered sacred.

Consort: an elvish mate. A term used exclusively by elves to refer to someone they are biologically compelled to pair up with. This usually involves intense sexual attraction, but can vary from person to person.

Demon: a being with horns or antlers, pointed ears, and symbiotic shadows. They are generally considered to be some of, if not *the* toughest beings in the world, as their shadows can make them almost indestructible. They are also naturally extremely strong and durable. Demon clans tend to be extremely close-knit, partially due to the fact that the world at large is not wholly accepting of them and their mythological connection to the god Blight. Identifying mating features are utter devotion, heightened protectiveness, and the sharing of shadows. This is when a mate is "given" a piece of the demon's symbiotic shadow, which will then live on that person for the rest of their life.

Dragon: a person with a dual form. In their bipedal form, they have claw-tipped wings, horns, and a tail. In their quadrupedal form, they are roughly the size of a standard SUV and can fly at extremely high altitudes for weeks at a time. They come in a variety of extremely saturated colors that shift with the time of day (light to dark). They breathe cold blue fire and can see the Earth's magnetic field. Identifying mating feature is marked change in behavior, including the overwhelming urge to nest.

Elemental: a being created by a spontaneous magical eruption. They often take on the attributes of whatever weather they happen to be born into, *i.e.* a lightning storm might produce a lightning elemental, or a blizzard might make a snow elemental.

Empath: a person with the ability to feel and manipulate the emotions of others.

Elf: someone born with jewel-toned skin, claws, pointed ears, and four fangs. Very secretive and considered apex predators who require a strict hierarchy to function. Average height of 6-7ft. Identifying mating feature is the retraction of claws.

Fever: shifter mating imperative triggered by the "animal's" choosing of a mate. Marked by a perpetual near-shift — elevated body temperature, increased aggression, build-up of magic, and the compulsion to mark. A shifter displays their readiness to find a mate by creating a den.

Fey: a person with nearly vestigial, insect-like wings, small fangs, and claws. Usually live in large groups. Identifying mating feature is bioluminescence.

Foresight: the ability to see multiple possible futures. The average number is between 2-4, with the likelihood mental instability increasing with each subsequent possible future.

Great War: a conflict between the territories of the North American continent that began in 1817 and ended in 1917 with the signing of the Peace Charter, which established the United Territories and Allies of modern times.

Halfling: the elvish term for an elf with mixed heritage.

Healer: a person who possesses the ability to see into and heal bodies through touch.

Isand: the title of the leader of the Draakonriik. Pronounced *ee-zah-nd*

M- : M- is frequently used as shorthand to denote when something is infused or otherwise combined with a magical element.

Marriage Sigil: a custom symbol branded into the foreheads of spouses (pairs or multiples). Each one is unique and infused with a small amount of magic as a reminder of the power love holds. They are typically sought out by worshippers of Glory — mainly witches and arrants. Elves, though worshippers, don't usually take a marriage sigil when they find their consorts or form a unions with other elves.

Mate: a catchall term for a significant other. Used by many cultures, it has varying degrees of weight. To shifters, orcs, and demons, the word mate is synonymous with family, monogamy, and dependence. It is much more loosely used within arrant society, as well as amongst elves, who generally prefer the term *consort.*

Merfolk: a catch-all term referring to sentient beings who live in the ocean, lakes, or rivers. Due to the nature of the ocean and its inhabitants, classifying all beings individually is almost impossible, so a much broader term is used to refer to both mammalian and non-mammalian beings than would be used for those on land.

Met: acronym for *magically enhanced tech.* A branded home assistant that can do everything your Alexa can, as well as small, low-level magic to help around the house.

Metallurgic Inoculation: a vaccine given to all elves within hours of birth to make them immune to iron poisoning.

M-siphon: a containment device used to imprison a magical being and siphon off their magic. Highly illegal.

R-siphon: also known as *reverse siphon.* New technology that redistributes magic away from the siphon instead of into it.

M-lev: a play on *maglev,* meaning a high speed train that levitates using magnets. In this case, magnets *and* magic.

M-weather: magic weather. Very common, but can result in "clusters" or storms that wreak havoc if not properly contained. In rare circumstances, it can also produce a sapient being known as an *elemental.*

Orc: a person with green, gray, russet, or blue skin, two fangs, and claws. Widely renowned for their strength and beautiful voices.

Identifying mating feature is "the kohl", or altered, dark pigmentation of the hands and feet developed after meeting their mate.

Pixie: a small, winged creature with compound eyes with about the same level of intelligence as a rat. In the wild they live in trees and in burrows, but have adapted to living in walls, pipes, mailboxes, etc.

Pull: elvish mating imperative. A sudden hormonal shift caused by exposure to a compatible partner's pheromones, marked by the retraction of claws and volatile mood shifts. The pull is only "satisfied" when hormone binding occurs — the term for long term exposure to a mate, resulting in permanent biological dependence on their pheromones. This process increases fertility and often results in the conception of multiples. Lack of exposure to a mate can cause severe physical reactions (lack of appetite, muscle pain, headaches, insomnia) as well as the deterioration of mental stability.

Shifter: a person who can shift into an animal form. They can partially shift (changing only parts of their bodies at will) and often take on characteristics of their other half. Famous for their strength and tenacity, as well as their dual-voiced "shifter purr" which many people find deeply attractive. Usually found in packs.

Sigil: a symbol used to channel magic. Western countries use the alchemical alphabet formally codified in the 1800's, though many, many variations are used all over the world.

Sovereign: the title of the ruler of the Elvish Protectorate. It is capitalized when used in place of a name.

Turbo Virgin (c): Theodore Thaddeus Solbourne, Sovereign of the Elvish Protectorate and Head of the Solbourne Family.

Union: an elvish marriage. Usually done for financial, political, or procreational benefit. The parties involved are not fated or biologically compelled to be with one another, and might have many lovers or even a consort outside of their union.

Vampire: a person who drinks blood to survive and cannot go out in sunlight. Vampirism can only be "caught" with the exchange of fresh blood, and as of 2045 is much more widely spread through procreation. Vampires can only breed with their *anchors.* Identifying mating feature is marked change in behavior, including overwhelming desire and need for total isolation.

Ward: a magical barrier with varying levels of protection. A ward can be something as simple as a proximity alert — "someone walked into my garden" — or as complex as full on defense — "someone crossed the threshold and has now burst into flames". The severity of the ward depends on the complexity of the sigils used to create them, and wards can have many layers, each one with a unique purpose. Personal wards can also be used, such as in clothing or embedded into jewelry, though they tend to be expensive and difficult to foolproof.

Were: a person infected with the were virus, a much mutated strain of the vampirism virus, resulting in altered physiology and magical ability. They can be identified by their heterochromia, or different colored eyes. They are the newest magical race and viewed warily by the general public for a variety of earned and unearned reasons. Identifying mating feature is marked change in behavior, including highly increased territorial instinct and the urge to nest. Pronounced *ware.*

Witch: Humans with the ability to use magic, which is passed down genetically. A person needs to be born with m-paths (a unique nervous system) to use it, however, humans were not initially adapted to use magic safely. Geneticists believe they acquired the ability through interbreeding with other beings. This interbreeding resulted in many unique qualities, such as the massive variety of abilities, power levels, and unique skills known to select families. However, it is also responsible for "burnout", which is the degenerative neurological condition a witch with mid-to-high level power will experience if they do not share their magical load with another being via witchbond. Witches are classified from least to most powerful — brightling, brilliant, and gloriana.

Witchbond: a magical bond formed between a witch and another being. Due to the nature of magic and humanity's much more recent adaptation to it, witches of *brilliant* and *gloriana* power must form a bond with another being usually beginning around 150-200 years old. This bond filters magic through the other being, neutralizing its damaging effects and reducing the chances of burnout to almost none. This bond also gives a power boost to the partner. A witchbond is permanent and can only be severed if one of the partners dies, at which point the surviving partner can form a new bond. Though commonly associated with a romantic partner, a witchbond is not inherently romantic and can be shared with a friend, sibling, or (ill-advised) an enemy.

Wraith: sentient shadow beings not dissimilar to elementals. They can affect the world around them in small ways, but can only speak to a very small number of demons. They lack physical forms but those that fully develop have complete sentience, personalities, and desires.

Content Warnings

Mass causality events, imprisonment, violence, isolation, religious themes, virginity, and sexual situations with a non-human character.

www.ingramcontent.com/pod-product-compliance
Lightning Source LLC
LaVergne TN
LVHW010659110826
845149LV00014B/3161